WATERSLAIN ANGELS

WATERSLAIN ANGELS

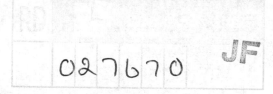

Kevin Crossley-Holland

GALAXY
PLUS

First published in Great Britain in 2008 by
Orion Children's Books
a division of the Orion Publishing Group
Ltd
This Large Print edition published
by BBC Audiobooks 2010
by arrangement with
the Orion Publishing Group Ltd

ISBN: 978 1405 664202

British Library Cataloguing in Publication Data available

Printed and bound in Great Britain by
CPI Antony Rowe, Chippenham and Eastbourne

For Jessica and Ashmole

AUTHOR'S NOTE
AND ACKNOWLEDGEMENTS

During the 1980s I lived in the Suffolk village of Walsham-le-Willows, where the angels are missing from the hammerbeam roof of the church. On a summer morning, a young woman brought me a Victorian newspaper report saying that one wing of one angel was on display in our own house, the Old Vicarage. My young daughters and I began to think and search . . . And that is how this book began.

Several kind people have assisted Annie and Sandy and their author during their quest for the missing Waterslain angels.

Jan Williams and Richard Barber both furnished me with material about William (Smasher) Dowsing, destroyer of so many angels and other 'monuments of idolatry and superstition' in East Anglian churches. Lynda Edwardes-Evans lent me books about honey bees, as well as a fascinating pollen colour guide, and generously combed my text for inaccuracies. Robert Rickett identified a mysterious wedge of wood, and William Heffer gave me copies of his dramatic photographs of Burnham Norton church, while Jane Wiederholt lifted a corner of the veil covering the mysteries of American Roman Catholic schooling.

Twiggy Bigwood has been a spirited and enterprising ally, deciphering my handwriting, typing many drafts, and researching hammerbeam roofs, G.I.s and Norfolk brides, well construction and other matters germane to the text. My editor and friend Judith Elliott, so liberal with her energy and enthusiasm, has once more given unstintingly of her experience, and her wise advice on characterisation and relationship has been just as crucial as her attention to minutiae. My wife Linda has not only commented line-by-line on the text but, as an American and ex-caver, she has helped me to shape the book's cross-currents as well as its underground scenes. For all this, and for her unwavering faith in this author, I am so grateful.

Chalk Hill, Burnham Market
February 2008

CHARACTERS

Annie Carter	*aged 10*
Margie Carter	*her mother*
Tom Carter	*her father*
Willa	*her half-sister*
Storm	*her nephew, aged 3*
Sandy Boroff	*aged 11*
Gracie Boroff (née Dune)	*his mother*
Revcrend Peter Potter	*rector of Waterslain*
Miss McQueen	*retired school teacher*
Alan Leppard	*garage mechanic*
Josie Sidebottom	*Sariel Chisel's aunt*
Peter Chisel	*wood carver, descendant of John Chisel*
Doctor Grant	*general practitioner*
The Bishop of Norwich	
William (Smasher) Dowsing's men	

Waterslain is a huddle of flint-and-chalk-and-brick cottages and outlying farms, with a round-towered church, on the north Norfolk coast. It stands on the edge of the wild saltmarshes, where samphire and sea-peas and purslane grow, and where at night the black dog Shuck and the ghost Storm roam. Although this village is no more than one hundred miles from London and the heart of the Midlands, it feels remote. This is partly because you can only travel to (and from) it, not through it, and also because the villagers have old stories and beliefs, and use their own local words. Waterslain is half-actual and half-imaginary.

Waterslain Angels takes place in 1955, two years after Queen Elizabeth's coronation, and ten years after the end of the Second World War. During this war, beaches, dunes and fields were strewn with rolls of barbed wire, concrete gun emplacements and the like, in case the Germans tried to land on the east coast of England.

Very many American troops were stationed at airbases in Norfolk and throughout East Anglia during and after the war, and no fewer than 30,000 Norfolk girls married U.S. servicemen. So there are still strong ties of family and friendship between East Anglians and Americans today.

1

On the edge of the marsh, there was a stand of poppies, poppies white as talcum powder and pink as peardrops and scarlet as new blood. The skins of their petals were so delicate. Annie was amazed at the way they withstood the withering wind that swayed the singing reeds and raced ripples down the black-and-silver creeks and rubbed salt into everyone and everything.

Poppies, thought Annie, they may look flimsy, but they're tough as old boots.

Old boots, as it happened, old Wellington boots were what Annie found as soon as she had crossed the saltmarsh and reached the beach. First she saw one lying in a warm rockpool, surrounded by dozens of nervy, see-through shrimps, and then she saw another standing on its own, jampacked with gravel. A third was sticking out of a hummock of dry sand, and Annie kicked at it just to make sure it wasn't attached to a body or anything. And then she found two more at the water's edge, with the sea dancing in them.

As Annie began to line these boots up, she realised with a shock that they were all for left feet.

Where have they come from, she wondered. Were they dumped off some ship? Who left them here? A troop of one-legged men?

Then Annie saw more boots were waiting for her in the marram clumps and the glistening saltstreams. And one she only rescued by wading into the water up to her waist. In all, she lined up twenty-eight Wellington boots—twenty-eight boots for left feet.

Offshore, shadows moved across the sunlit water. They grew towards Annie like spreading dark sails, like underwater shapes, she didn't know what. Then they passed right through her and Annie was left in sunlight again, standing on one leg and shivering.

Living in Waterslain is weird, thought Annie. I mean weird things happen and it's full of weird people. Old Rachel has a moustache and catches her breakfast in the creek with her toes, and the beachcomber Jessie says his shoulder bag's full of sunlight and moonlight. Moonshine, more like. And everyone still keeps talking about the Great Flood, and how water poured in through keyholes, and chained bulls were up to their necks and almost drowned.

And then, thought Annie, some people in Waterslain are more dead than alive, and they move around like sloths. Actually, I think this is a village where no one ever forgets anything and no one ever goes away, even when they die. I mean, what about those two soldiers who were drowned in Dead Man's Pool? Everyone still talks about them. And sometimes I can see the rotting corpse swinging on top of Gallow Hill, and his eyes have been pecked out, and he stares right through me. And what about the rector who lived around here and used to preach from inside a lion's cage, until the lions got fed up and ate him? If that's not weird, I don't know what is.

As Annie picked her way home along the cockle-path, wearing a black boot on her left hand like a giant's glove, she knew her mother would be

2

impatient.

'I told you an hour at the most,' complained Mrs Carter, tapping the top of Annie's head with her wooden stirring spoon. 'Your dad wants to go up to the hall.'

'That's why I didn't hurry,' Annie replied.

'Come on,' Mrs Carter said.

'A load of old junk,' said Annie.

'Don't spoil things for him. Anyhow, it might be interesting.'

'Like cows can fly,' Annie retorted.

'You don't know,' Mrs Carter said. 'You never can tell. In any case, he's put in the old windlass and bucket from our well.'

'I wish it still worked,' said Annie. 'Our well.'

'And the black snuff-box,' Mrs Carter went on. 'The one I had from my mother when she died, with Admiral Nelson's face on it.'

'You told me that before,' said Annie, waving the Wellington boot on her left hand.

'Take that out of my face,' exclaimed Mrs Carter, and she grabbed the end of the boot and pulled it off.

Annie grinned. 'It's for the show.'

'What nonsense you do talk.'

'There are twenty-seven more out there, and they're all left-footed.'

Mrs Carter snorted. 'Talk,' she said, 'and make up.'

'There are!' protested Annie.

Since he'd had his stroke three years before, when he was only thirty, Mr Carter had only been able to get around on sticks, so he and Annie had to drive up to the village hall although it was less than a mile away.

'What's this show about, anyway?' Annie asked him.

'Our village, Annie,' her father replied. 'Our village is telling its own story.'

'How?'

'Through bits and pieces. Through evidence, you'd call it, if you were a detective.'

'Like what?'

'You'll see,' Mr Carter told her.

'You could put this old car in,' suggested Annie. 'It's old enough. Half bald on the inside, grey on the outside.'

'My Hillman Imp,' said Mr Carter solemnly, 'me and my Hillman are indi . . . indi . . .'

'You always say that.'

'I always try to,' Mr Carter replied. 'Some words I can't get my tongue round. Not since my stroke.'

'You can,' said Annie. 'The ones that matter, you can.'

There was a power of people in the village hall. At least twenty. And the show wasn't as boring as Annie had expected. There was the unexploded bomb the Germans had dropped on the beach, now defused, and a hideous-looking gas mask, and a map showing how much land had been swallowed by the sea during the last five hundred years, and Edwardian parasols, and Victorian games and silver coins, as well as a little statue of a half-naked lady sitting on a rock; and there were all kinds of mementoes of Admiral Nelson, England's greatest naval hero, who had been born at Burnham Thorpe only a couple of miles away, and who had often walked over to Waterslain to watch the barges sailing in and out of the creek and tying up at the staithe.

4

'Look!' said Mr Carter. 'Here your mother's snuff-box.'

'That's odd, seeing it here,' Annie replied. 'As if it doesn't belong to us anymore.'

There was a piece of paper next to the snuff-box, with spindly words on it, written in black ink:

Pastures soaked with moon-white dew.
Dear Waterslain. The holy view.
Let me hear my childhood bells.

The saltmarsh silver-grey and bleak,
And a fresh tide swarming into the creek.
Reek of herring and tar and rope
And the island lanced by golden hope.
Let me hear my childhood bells.

The great gong tolling atop the lane,
And barges set for the staithe again.
Let me hear my childhood bells.'

'Who wrote that, then?' asked Annie.

Tom Carter shrugged. 'That's old-fashioned writing,' he said.

'It's true,' observed Annie, 'about everything being silvery-grey and then the island's suddenly lit up and golden. What does "childhood bells" mean?'

Mr Carter slowly shook his head. 'I think it's about remembering,' he replied.

'Like we all are,' said a voice in Annie's ear.

Annie gave a start. 'Oh!' she exclaimed. 'Mr Pitter.'

'Potter,' said the rector, smiling. He was pink as a baby and hadn't got much hair, but his eyebrows

5

made up for that. They were red and bushy, and the right one kept twitching.

'Yes,' said the Reverend Potter. 'We're all remembering in here. Remembering all the ages of Waterslain. Have you seen my wing?'

Annie stared at the Reverend Potter, amazed. His wing?

Mr Potter smiled. 'You look as if you've seen a ghost.'

'I have, actually,' said Annie. 'Anyhow, you haven't got a wing.'

'Not of my own,' the Reverend Potter agreed. 'I'd have to be an angel for that. Well, half-an-angel!' The rector took Annie's arm and the two of them shuffled along to the next showcase.

'Oh!' cried Annie. 'Dad! Where are you?'

There, in front of her, lay the most beautiful wing. A right wing. It was made of lots of little wooden struts or paddles shaped to look like feathers, all of them overlapping, and the longest ones curved and stretching out to the wing-tip.

'It's beautiful,' breathed Annie. 'Dad!' she called out again. 'Where are you?'

'Do you see how some of the feathers are still vermilion?' the rector asked.

'What's that?'

'Bright red. Scarlet.'

'They're not really,' said Annie.

'No, well, they've faded. But that's the original paint, all right, five hundred years old.'

'Some are marsh-green,' said Annie.

'That's original too,' the rector told her. 'And the brownish feathers were once painted yellowy-orange. Ochre.'

Annie couldn't take her eyes off the wing.

6

'Where does it come from?' she asked.

'Where do you suppose?'

Annie looked up. Her eyes were round and dark as two Nelson snuff-boxes.

'It doesn't!' she exclaimed.

The Reverend Potter nodded and his right eyebrow worked overtime. 'From our church roof,' he said. 'Our own church roof. It must do.'

'How did you get it?' Annie demanded.

'Alan Leppard was clearing out my attic last week. He's been doing odd jobs for me and my wife, and he found it right at the back. Jammed behind the chimney breast. It must have been there for generations.'

'Wow!' exclaimed Annie.

'Good thing I went up there when I did,' the Reverend Potter told her. 'Alan said he was just about to chuck it out with all the rubbish.'

'Where's the left wing, then?'

The rector shook his head.

'And all the others?'

'I don't know any more than you do, Annie. No more than it says on this note here. Look!'

The Reverend Potter peered into the showcase, and screwed up his eyes a bit. 'You read it,' he told her.

'There were once fourteen angels . . .' Annie began, but then she stopped. 'Fourteen!' she exclaimed.

'What's so strange about that?' asked the rector.

'Twice fourteen is twenty-eight,' she said, frowning. And there were twenty-eight boots on the beach, she thought. I said Waterslain is weird.

'True enough,' said the rector. 'And there are four rows of seven feathers on each wing, and four

7

sevens are twenty-eight. So what do you make of that?'

'Weird,' said Annie.

'Go on, then,' said the rector.

'There were once fourteen angels,' Annie began again, 'in the hammerbeam roof of Waterslain church. The angels in many East Anglian churches were destroyed during the Ref . . .'

'Reformation,' said the rector. 'During the Reformation and the time of Cromwell.'

'There's a strong belief in the village,' Annie read, 'that our angels were hidden to save them but that, years later, no one could remember where. What is certain is that the name of the woodcarver who made the angels, and how much he was paid, is recorded in the business accounts in the Black Book in the church. He was one John Chisel, and, after five hundred years, some of his descendants still live in Norfolk.'

Annie looked up at the Reverend Potter. 'Did you write that?' she asked.

'I did.'

'Is it still there? The Black Book?'

'It certainly is.'

'Can I see it?'

The rector shook his head and closed his eyes. 'The Black Book's locked in the vestry chest,' he said. 'One day, maybe, Annie. Now have a good look round, won't you.'

'I'm going to find our angels,' Annie told him. 'I am. I'm going to find out where they were hidden.'

At this moment, Annie's father swung round the corner of the showcase on his sticks. Then Annie saw he was talking to a boy and a woman, and he was grinning from ear to ear.

'By all the angels in heaven!' Mr Carter exclaimed.

Annie looked puzzled.

'Annie,' her father said. 'This is Sandy.'

Annie stared at Sandy. She thought she had never seen such a delicate creature in all her life. He had fine hair as sandy as his name, and spectacles with rims so thick they looked more like goggles, and his skin was pale and shiny, even slightly pearly, like the inside of a mussel shell.

'Hi!' said Sandy.

'Hello,' said Annie cautiously.

'And this is Gracie,' Tom Carter went on, quite unable to stop smiling. 'My! Oh my! Who'd have thunk I'd ever see Gracie Dune again?'

'Boroff,' the woman corrected him. 'Gracie Boroff.'

'I know,' said Mr Carter.

Gracie Boroff nodded pleasantly at Annie. 'You all right, then?' she asked.

Gracie was blonde. Her hair was as rough as a rook's nest, her clothes were too tight-fitting, and she was quite brassy. In fact, thought Annie, she looks as if she's stepped out of one of those naughty postcards.

'Gracie's just back from the U. S. of A.,' her father told Annie. 'But you're a Waterslain girl, aren't you, Gracie?'

'Will you let me speak for myself, Tom Carter?'

'You never had no trouble with that.'

Gracie smiled gaily, and light danced in her hazel-and-green eyes. 'Still the same old Tommy,' she said.

'Wish I was,' said Mr Carter. 'Not since my stroke.'

'I heard about that,' Gracie said. 'And very sorry I was.' She draped an arm round Tom Carter's shoulder. 'And you . . . you heard about Bruce?'

'We did,' said Mr Carter.

'Bruce was Sandy's dad,' Gracie told Annie. 'Bruce Boroff.'

Annie didn't know quite what to say. She was thinking Gracie wore much too much eye-liner.

Gracie Boroff took a deep breath and ballooned her cheeks and squirted out all the air. 'The point is, Sandy and I have come back to live in Waterslain.'

'Quite right too,' said Mr Carter.

Sandy stood very still. Behind his spectacles, he blinked.

Gracie smiled at Annie. 'Your dad and I were at school together. Here, and then in Lynn. We always sat on the train together.'

'Gracie!' said Tom Carter.

'Well, we did, didn't we, Tommy?'

Annie made a face at her father. She wasn't sure she really wanted to know.

'That's enough, Gracie,' Tom Carter said.

Annie inspected Sandy. 'Are you coming to school, then?'

'We don't know yet,' his mother jumped in. 'Sandy's always gone to Catholic school but there isn't one near here. The closest is in Dereham, and that's twenty miles away.'

'But aren't Catholic schools the same as normal schools?' asked Annie.

'Oh no!' said Gracie. 'At Catholic school, the teachers are penguins.'

'Penguins!'

'Well, nuns. But that's what all the sisters look

10

like. Sister Mercedes and Sister Winifred and Sister Generose. All of them. Sandy's very clever, though, so he had extra lessons in math and history and Latin from Father Gabriel.'

'Who?'

'Father Gabriel. He was our priest.'

Annie glanced at Sandy. He looked so weedy that she wondered whether he'd get bullied and broken to pieces.

'How old are you?' she asked him.

'Eleven,' said Sandy.

'Eleven!' exclaimed Annie, and then she blushed. 'I mean . . . well, you don't look older than me.'

'It's all right,' said Sandy.

'Yes,' said Gracie Boroff. 'You're both war babies.'

Annie suddenly felt sorry for Sandy—sorry because he had such a noisy mother, sorry because he looked like such a dismal shrimp.

'Have you seen the wing?' she asked him.

Sandy blinked.

'The angel's wing?'

'Nope.'

'It's amazing.'

Then Annie led Sandy round to the showcase with the angel's wing in it, and she just wondered for a moment whether it would still be there.

Gracie Boroff sighed. 'You'll help me, won't you, Tommy? If your Annie could take him under her wing.'

'You know kids,' Tom Carter said with a shrug. 'You know what they're like.'

'But you'll have a word with her,' Gracie said.

'That's up to her,' Tom Carter replied.

11

When they got home, Annie wanted to tell her mother about the amazing wing and the American boy, and her father wanted to tell her about Gracie . . .

'That piece of work!' exclaimed Mrs Carter.

'Margie!' said Mr Carter.

'Throwing herself at all the G.I.s.'

'That's history,' said Mr Carter. 'Anyhow, you know he was killed.'

'Who?' asked Annie.

'Gracie's husband,' her father replied. 'Bruce Boroff. B'off! That's what we called him.'

'Tom!' objected Mrs Carter.

'B'off and F'off! Boroff and Flintoff. Strutting around, the two of them, handing out chocolates and cigarettes and bars of soap, chatting up the girls. Yes,' her father told Annie, 'Bruce was a pilot, and he got killed, flying a mission after the war was over. Anyhow, Annie, you and Sandy . . .'

'What?' Annie asked suspiciously.

'He could come round ours.'

'Why?'

'You could show him the marsh.'

'I don't think so,' said Annie.

'No,' said Mr Carter. 'No, well, he is rather a miserable specimen. Gracie would be pleased, though.'

Annie wrinkled up her nose. 'He's half-transparent,' she said. 'More like an elf than a human boy.'

'That woman!' Margie Carter complained. 'Turning up like a bad penny. I thought we'd seen the back of her.'

2

The ladder was so long. So heavy. Really, it needed two people to carry it.

By mistake Annie banged the leading end into the oak door, and the door swung open, and if the congregation had been inside, they would have thought it was Doomsday.

Inside the gloomy church, Annie tried to swing the ladder round, but then she tripped on the hem of her nightie. She staggered, and the back end of the ladder swiped all the leaflets off the table inside the door.

Annie dragged the ladder across the polished tiles, and it left two dirty lines. But all the same, she somehow managed to lean it against the pulpit, and slowly push it upright. Then, holding it in front of her, she waltzed it across to the flinty church wall. She could hear how loudly she was panting.

Only then did Annie realise there were other people in the church. She couldn't see them, but she could hear them. The whisperers.

'Smasher . . .'

'Smasher says the stone dish, you know, the water stoup . . .'

'And the big painting, the one of Mary suckling baby Jesus.'

'Smasher says don't forget the roof angels.'

'The roof angels, yes.'

'Get them. Gut them. Hack them into pieces.'

'How will we get up there?'

'What if there isn't a ladder?'

13

'Shoot at them. Pepper them. Puncture them like colanders.'

'Blow their eyes out.'

Annie knew she had to rescue the roof angels, and she knew how little time there was. So little time before the whisperers started their foul work.

As she began to scale the long ladder, it seemed to Annie that she was climbing from darkness to light. From earth to heaven, almost. She rose above the pews, above the pretty pulpit from which the Reverend Potter preached each Sunday, above the old stone tablets affixed to the wall, above the leaded windows . . .

The ladder quivered. Once it shuddered, and Annie gripped the bar in front of her nose very tightly, and moaned.

Below her, she could hear the whisperers, the whisperers. And above her, she could hear a strange trembling, singing sound, all on one high note, a sort of crying that hadn't broken into tears.

'Smasher says . . .'

'We'll never reach them.'

'Not up there.'

'We need a ladder.'

Annie held her breath. She held it for so long she was afraid she would gasp out loud.

Up she climbed. Up. But when she reached the very top rung, and stood with her palms pressed against the sharp, flinty wall, Annie realised her ladder wasn't long enough. She still couldn't reach the first roof angel.

Annie shivered. She had strained every sinew and fallen short. She had failed the angels, and she knew the time of Eden had come to an end and the time of evil had begun.

14

'Look!'

'There's a ladder!'

'Over there?'

'God provides!'

'We'll get them.'

'And gut them.'

'We'll hack them into pieces.'

Up the ladder swarmed the dark whisperers. They still hadn't seen Annie standing at the top.

Annie looked up into the face of the angel just above her. True, it wasn't wearing goggles but there was no mistaking him. None at all. It was Sandy.

3

Next morning, Annie had to go to the dentist. Her mother always made an appointment right at the beginning of the summer and winter holidays 'to get it over with'. And after lunch, it being Monday, Annie had to help her mother put the washing through the mangle. Then Annie's old schoolteacher, Miss McQueen, came to give Annie her weekly piano lesson, and her weekly ticking off for not practising often enough.

But Annie's dark dream stayed with her all day, and at the end of the afternoon she decided to go up to the church to see whether there was any sign of the angels or the whisperers.

There's no point asking Polly or Daisy to come, thought Annie, or any other of my friends. They wouldn't really be interested.

Surrounded by summer's waving grasses, with their pale stems and nodding mauve heads, Waterslain church looked quite embedded. Almost as if it's grown out of the ground, thought Annie. Green with lichen, white with sea-salt and grey with age.

Annie picked her way from grave to grave, reading bits of the inscriptions. She didn't know what she was looking for. She just knew she wanted to find out more about the wing, more about the missing angels.

Lots of the tombstones were carved with names Annie recognised—Haines and Riches and Leppard and Scoles and Chisel and Mason and Thompson—and a few of them said things about angels. In death, Susie Leppard was one with 'angel-voices ever singing', and in life Amy Croft had possessed 'such angel grace', and Henry Beecher, who died when he was only six, was now 'a holy angel bright'.

Where does all this get me, thought Annie. Anyhow, what is an angel exactly?

She looked up at the round tower, almost one thousand years old, and with its eight small dark eyes the tower looked south and east and west across green-and-gold Norfolk and north across the saltmarsh to the shining blade of the sea.

Annie went on picking and poking her way around the churchyard. She made a daisy chain. She inspected the old graves of the ships' captains who lived at the same time as Admiral Nelson, and in Victorian times, when big ships, bursting with grain and malt and coal, still used to sail up to the staithe. Then she came across a tombstone that just had one word on it.

GONE!

Above the word there was a closed stone hand with its forefinger pointing toward heaven, and when Annie looked more closely, she saw there had once been words near the bottom of the stone. But the wind had sandpapered them and although she scratched at them a bit with her penknife, she couldn't make them out.

Gone, thought Annie. Gone but not gone. Like the angels. I'm going to find them, I am.

When Annie looked up at the church again, she saw the dark little panes in the leaded south window were glinting and flashing, as if the church were packed with people and each of them was waving a sparkler.

17

Annie had heard of the phantom congregation, all right, but she wasn't afraid of them. Not her. A couple of years before, when she was eight, she'd met the ghost of the old farmer killed by the highwaymen. She actually rode with him on his horse round the edge of the marsh in the middle of the night, that night when she had to fetch Doctor Grant because her half-sister Willa had gone into labour.

There's no harm in phantoms, Annie thought to herself. You can't harm them and they can't harm you.

Her mother agreed. 'You won't even see them unless you want to,' she said. 'The only harm in Waterslain church is up in the old tower. Wild bees swarmed there just after the war, and they've been there ever since. They buzz and fizz like nobody's business, and if you bother them, they'll sting you to death in two minutes.'

'Really?' said Annie.

'Little howitzers!'

'What?'

'Buzz-bombs,' Mrs Carter told her. 'Now, Annie! Promise me you won't go anywhere near the church. Not on your own.'

'Promise!' said Annie.

One wall of the porch was deeply scored with four long gouges, as if a witch had torn at the limestone with her fingernails. Annie didn't like looking at them, so she walked quickly up to the small door cut into the big old oak door, and lifted the latch.

Inside the quiet church, Annie immediately looked up into the towering oak roof.

Hammerbeam. That's what the note in the

18

village hall called it, the one about the angel's wing. Hammerbeam. Whatever that meant.

The angels weren't there. Of course they weren't.

Annie stretched back her neck until it made her shoulders ache and she looked like a girl in a medieval painting. She stared at the oak stars that had once shone above each angel's head. A few were still as brown as onion-skins, the same colour as some of the feathers in the angel's wing. Then she gazed at the small dark holes in the beams.

Annie saw that little round pegs were sticking out of two of the holes, and she cried out in delight. There they still were after hundreds of years, the pegs that had once fitted into a hole in an angel's back.

'It's like they're waiting!' she exclaimed.

At this moment, Annie heard a hollow thump. It came from inside the pulpit, and it wasn't a sound that angels make, angels or phantoms or wild bees or even the church's ancient heating system.

The little bones in Annie's neck cricked and cracked. She stood absolutely still. Then there was a pulpit-sniff. In fact, it was more of a snort.

'Who's there?' demanded Annie. Her voice sounded twice as loud as she meant it to be, as though she were speaking into her Great Auntie Tilly's ear-trumpet.

Slowly a figure appeared out of the pulpit, rising from it like a column of smoke. It had sandy hair and spectacles, and was wearing a T-shirt.

'You again!' exclaimed Annie. 'What are you doing?'

'Thinking.'

'It's a good thing Pitterpatter didn't catch you

19

up there.'

'Who?'

'Pitterpatter. The Reverend Potter.' Annie grinned. 'He'd have your guts for garters.'

Sandy's eyes gleamed behind his specs. 'In that case,' he said, 'I'd have stayed . . . invisible.'

'Thinking about what?' asked Annie.

'Same as you,' said Sandy.

'How do you know?'

'Because,' said Sandy. 'Because I'm a wise old owl.' He cupped his hands to his mouth and hooted, and the sound echoed all round the church.

'Ssshhh!'

Sandy stared down at Annie. 'Alone and warming his five wits, the white owl in the pulpit sits.'

'You're weird,' said Annie.

'Wings and things,' said Sandy. 'I was thinking about the angels.'

'So was I.'

'There you go,' said Sandy. 'I told you so.'

'Are you coming down or what?' asked Annie.

Sandy descended the little wooden steps. 'Actually,' he said, 'I think it goes "in the belfry sits" but it doesn't matter. I've decided to find them.'

'What?'

'The angels.'

Annie stared at Sandy. 'La dee da,' she said.

'You don't understand. I gotta find them.'

'Why?'

'Because of my dad.'

'What do you mean?'

Sandy blinked.

'What does your dad have to do with angels?'

'I'll tell you sometime,' said Sandy awkwardly.

Annie frowned. 'Find them where, anyhow?'

'That's what I was thinking about. I'll find them inside my head.' Sandy reached into one pocket of his grey shorts and pulled out a packet. 'Want one?'

'What is it?'

'What's it look like?'

'A cigarette.'

'Barratt's,' said Sandy. 'Call yourself English and you don't know Barratt's.'

'Twice as English as you are,' said Annie. She helped herself to one of the sticky sweet white cigarettes and put it between her lips. Sandy reached forward and, with a click of his tongue, pretended to light up the red end, and then lit up his own.

Sandy spread his arms. 'This place is cool.'

'It always is in summer,' Annie replied.

'Whaddya mean?'

'It is,' said Annie. 'Not in winter, though. Not when the old heater cranks into action. It clanks and bangs while Pitterpatter's preaching, and the heat blasts up through these grilles.'

'I get you,' said Sandy. 'No, I mean cool, like, neat! I've never been in a building half this old before. In the U.S., all the churches are new.'

'Weird,' said Annie.

'And they're busy,' Sandy went on. 'Meetings, Sunday school, the kitchen, the coffee room, people all over the shop.'

'Coffee room,' exclaimed Annie. 'In a church?'

'Yeah.'

Annie shook her head. 'It sounds more like the

21

village hall.'

'Boy!' said Sandy. 'It sure is quiet in here. Silent as the grave.'

Still smoking their sweet cigarettes, Annie and Sandy both stared up into the hammerbeam roof.

It feels like the angels are still here, thought Annie. They are! They're here but we can't see them.

Side by side the two of them gazed.

And if I keep looking like this, thought Annie, somehow I'll bring them back again.

'This roof's a hull,' Sandy said in a thoughtful voice. 'The hull of a huge open boat.'

'Set for the staithe again,' Annie replied, remembering the poem in the village hall.

'No,' said Sandy. 'Upside down. We gotta consider every clue. We mustn't leave one stone unturned.'

Annie didn't ask him what he was talking about. What makes him so sure I'm ready to share my angels with him, she wondered.

'You know what Mom says,' Sandy went on, still gazing up at the roof. 'If you want to find the pot of gold, you've got to turn over every stone in the field. It's always under the last one.'

'I know that story,' Annie said.

'It isn't a story.'

'It is, actually,' said Annie in a matter-of-fact voice.

Sandy turned to look at her, and his sweet cigarette dropped from his mouth and fell through the bars of the metal grille into the hellfire heating system below.

'No!' exclaimed Annie. 'Now the furnace probably won't work.'

22

Sandy wrinkled his nose.

'You've probably gummed it up.'

'Cool!' said Sandy. 'Cool in summer, cool in winter! Look at this.' He pulled a postcard out of the pocket of his shirt.

'What is it?' asked Annie.

'About the angels.'

There was no picture. Just a few words about oak pegs and fledglings and battle-lights . . .

Annie stared at them and shook her head. 'It's too difficult,' she said.

'Because you're trying to eat it all in one mouthful,' Sandy said. 'Anyhow, it's a clue.' He slotted the card back into his pocket.

'Where did you get it?' Annie asked.

'By the door. There's a pile of them.'

'Free?'

Sandy shrugged. 'So what.' He put his hands deep into his pockets and padded down the nave, whistling.

When I first saw him, thought Annie, I told Mum his skin was pale as the inside of a mussel. But it's not really. It's almost transparent, except you can't see the inside of him. It's as gauzy as the wing of a lacewing.

'What's it like?' Sandy asked. 'Waterslain.'

Annie stuck out her lower lip. 'Normal for Norfolk,' she said.

'I guess,' said Sandy. 'It's a bit of a dump.'

Annie stared at Sandy. 'A fat lot you know about it,' she replied.

'Go on, then,' said Sandy.

But Annie didn't. She didn't see why she should.

'It's Mom who wanted to come back across the pond,' Sandy told her.

23

'What pond?' asked Annie.

'The Atlantic, dumb-bell! Ever since Dad . . . She says the U.S. never suited her. Keeps saying she wants a new beginning.'

'A new old beginning, you mean,' said Annie.

'Back to her roots,' said Sandy. 'All that stuff.'

'And you wanted to stay put,' said Annie. It was more of a statement than a question.

Sandy looked at Annie through his goggles. 'Mom says it'll be tough to begin with—you know, making new friends.'

Annie understood. At least, she could hear how anxious Sandy was.

'Do you know about flying angel?' Sandy asked her in a serious voice.

Annie shook her head.

'Angel height?'

'No.'

'You seen *Angels One Five*?'

Annie frowned.

'You haven't? It's a film about the Battle of Britain. It's what airmen call it—flying angel, angel height—when they're at one thousand feet.'

'Why angel?' asked Annie.

'Because it's . . . I don't know, quite close to heaven. That's what Mom says.'

'And close to earth as well,' said Annie. 'One thousand feet. That's only three hundred and thirty-three yards.'

'Are you a math wizard or something?'

'It's my best subject,' said Annie.

'Mine too. Math and English, Father Gabriel said.'

'One thousand feet. Only three times as long as the football pitch. Well, and a bit.'

24

'Soccer, you mean,' said Sandy.

'When planes from Sculthorpe come over that low,' Annie went on, 'you can read the marking on their wings, and the sky goes on roaring and shaking for hours.'

'It all seems more real on this side of the pond,' Sandy said. He swallowed. 'My dad disappeared when he was flying angel.'

'Disappeared?' repeated Annie.

'He crashed into the ocean. His body was never found.'

'Oh!' cried Annie. 'I didn't know!'

'I'm only just getting used to things over here,' Sandy said quietly. 'Those gun-emplacements in the middle of fields . . .'

'Pill-boxes, you mean?'

'Yeah, and the rolls of barbed wire on the beach. And the huge metal spikes to stop the Germans being able to land.'

'Why?' asked Annie. 'Aren't there any in America?'

'In the U. S. of A,' said Sandy, 'people went away to war . . .'

'Lots came here,' said Annie.

'Exactly,' Sandy went on. 'So there were no signs of the war like there are here.'

'Did you live in a place like Waterslain?'

'Hell, no,' said Sandy. 'We lived in an apartment.'

'What's that?'

'A flat. In a city. I'd never seen the sea before I came to England.'

Sandy strolled over to the little organ and lifted the lid. He pressed down a few of the silent keys.

'Wanna put some puff into it?' he asked Annie.

25

'What?'
'Blow the bellows.'
'It's not allowed.'
'Says who?'

Annie pointed to a small white card affixed to the front of the organ.

VISITORS ARE KINDLY
REQUESTED TO REFRAIN FROM
TOUCHING THE ORGAN

'Says words!' scoffed Sandy. 'Says long words. Go on.'

Annie smiled. Feeling a bit nervous in case Pitterpatter should walk in, she grasped the wooden handle on the side of the organ and began to pump it up and down, as if she were pumping the handle above the washboard in the kitchen— easy to begin with, then stiffer, until at last water erupted from the old tap, in bursts at first, then in a steady, shining flow.

The organ wheezed, it grunted, and Sandy began to play. With his right hand he picked out the first bars of a hymn, whistling softly as he did so. C-E-C-G-E-C. A long note, that last C. And then, B-A-G-F-E-D. When he played the last D, Sandy played B as well, and left both fingers on the keys.

'I know that,' exclaimed Annie. 'Ye holy angels

bright . . .'

'Assist our song,' Sandy went on. 'Assist our song! We need all the help we can get.'

'Once you start looking for them, there are angels everywhere,' said Annie.

Now Sandy started to play strange, drifty music. He closed his eyes.

'Lost notes,' said Annie. 'That's what they sound like.'

'Sympathetic magic,' Sandy replied.

'What's that?'

'I can't explain it,' said Sandy. 'Sort of understanding. Sort of inviting.'

'Inviting the angels, you mean—in case they want to be found.'

'Something like that.'

Yes, thought Annie. He's like a shrimp, somehow. I can almost see through him.

4

'You're too headstrong by half,' stormed Mrs Carter. 'The second day of the holidays, and you're already getting under my skin.'

Annie held her ground and looked up at her mother, unblinking. 'Please!'

'I've told you. No! Your father's feeling too poorly to drive and I've got dozens of things to do. The ironing, for starters.'

Annie stared at her mother under her mop of dark brown hair. 'This is important,' she said doggedly.

'For the love of mike, Annie, go out on the marsh or something.'

'It's pelting,' said Annie.

'Go and see Polly or Daisy, then.'

'They wouldn't be interested.'

'Dear Lord,' said Mrs Carter, 'there's more to life than angels.'

Annie grasped the steel bar of the Aga cooker and squeezed it. 'I'll walk there, then,' she said in a very deliberate voice.

'You'll do no such thing,' Mrs Carter replied. 'What's got into you?'

Annie glared at her mother.

'Come on, now, young lady. Help me with some ironing, and if your father's feeling better, maybe we can drive over to South Creake later.'

Now and then, as they sprinkled and ironed and folded all the weekly washing, Mrs Carter sneaked a look at Annie, who was very quiet and contained, as though her body were in the cottage kitchen but her head was somewhere else altogether. How determined she is, thought Mrs Carter. Once she gets an idea into her head, there's no stopping her.

'I like my best blouse,' Annie observed, running her fingers down the panel of tiny, stitched flower-heads covering the buttons.

'Yarroway,' her mother said.

'What-a-what?' asked Annie.

'Yarroway. It's on all the verges. White. Pinkish too.'

Annie nodded.

'It's called angel-flower as well,' Mrs Carter told her, smiling.

'Mum! Are you having me on?'

'I do know,' her mother replied, 'that if you stuff it up your nose, that'll give you a nosebleed. Me and your Aunt Rose did that, and we sang, "Yarroway, yarroway, bear a white blow. If my love love me, my nose will bleed now"'

'What's a white blow?' asked Annie.

Mrs Carter shook her head. 'I'm blowed if I know!' she replied. 'Thank you, dear. Thanks for helping me. We'll see if we can drive out later.'

July rain was spitting at the small panes. And now and then the east wind gave them a good shaking.

When Annie looked in on her father in the sitting-room, she saw he was snoozing in his rocking-chair. At least, his eyes were closed, and that meant he didn't want to be disturbed. Annie crept over to the shelf, pulled out the tatty old book on wildflowers, and walked sedately out of the room again. She climbed the stairs to her own little room and threw herself down on the rag rug.

When she found the entry for yarrow, Annie

realised her mother hadn't told her everything, not by a long chalk. Yarrow, she read, makes a woman's figure sweeter and her voice gladder, and her lips like the juice of strawberry . . . Annie savoured the entry again. How does it do all that, she wondered.

The longer Annie looked at the wildflower book, the more she found. And after an hour, she had picked a whole spray of angels! Angel's Trumpets and Angel's Eyes which, she read, is another name for trembling speedwell; Archangels, which are white and yellow dead-nettles; Angels and Devils; and even Angel's Pincushions . . .

Annie listed the wildflowers in her notebook one by one. Quite what use they'll be, she thought, I've no idea. I don't know whether or not they've got anything to do with my angels. But Sandy's right. Well, Sandy's mum. You've got to turn over every stone in the field.

That afternoon, Mr Carter felt more himself, and the weather cleared up a bit, so the three of them did drive out after all, but not before Mrs Carter had exasperated her husband and Annie by having 'just one more thing to do' upstairs.

Twice Mr Carter rapped the ceiling with his stick, the second time quite irritably.

'Can't you make her hurry?' asked Annie.

'I've been married to the woman for eleven years,' her father replied, 'and she's never once failed to keep me waiting.'

Mrs Carter clattered down the steep wooden stairs. 'What's worthwhile is worth waiting for,' she said, beaming and patting herself. 'You do always hurry me, Tom.'

'Now where shall we go?' asked Mr Carter, as soon as they were ensconced in the Hillman Imp.

'Dad!' complained Annie in a reproachful voice. 'South Creake.'

'Yes, yes,' said Mr Carter. He turned to Annie's mother. 'Our Annie's really caught the angel-bug.'

'Talking of angels,' Mrs Carter said in a lemon voice, 'I hear Gracie's wings are already dropping off.'

Annie pricked up her ears. But her father frowned and shook his head.

'I'll tell you later,' his wife added.

'She's a rough old diamond,' Tom Carter replied.

In the diamond-shaped field behind the Carters' cottage, the ears of wheat were ripe but the half nearer to the marsh looked more grey than gold.

'That's the Flood,' Mr Carter said, more to himself than to his wife or daughter. 'Half escaped, half didn't. That'll take another year to wash out all the salt.'

All around, there were still signs of the Great Flood that had lacerated Waterslain two years before. Gaps in hedges. Breached dykes filled with thousands of sandbags. Wavy watermarks on walls. The limestone marker on the watermill showing how high the floodwater had risen when the stream began to flow inland and not out to sea.

'The Advertiser says there's to be a memorial in Hunst'n,' Mr Carter said.

'What's that for, then?' asked his wife.

'The drowned Americans. You know, the servicemen trying to rescue people.'

'And their wives,' Mrs Carter added.

'And their wives,' Mr Carter echoed her.

31

'Norfolk was like a war zone.'

Mrs Carter nodded. 'It was,' she said, and she gave a deep sigh. 'All over again.'

'What was he like?' asked Annie from the back of the car.

'What was who like?' her mother said.

'Sandy's dad. Bruce Boroff.'

'Bruce,' replied Mrs Carter. 'Big man. Big smile. Lovely brown eyes. Booming voice.'

'Not like Sandy, then.'

'Not in the least, no. Well, he did have sandy hair.'

'Can you go a bit faster, Dad?' Annie asked.

'No.'

'The angels are getting impatient.'

Mr Carter gave his daughter a knowing look in the rearview mirror. 'Imps aren't made for speed,' he said.

'29mph!' protested Annie. 'You never go more than 29.'

'So we can see the world,' her father replied.

'It's weird, anyhow,' Annie said. 'A grey Imp searching for angels.'

As soon as Mr Carter reached South Creake and pulled up in Church Lane, Annie jumped out. 'See you inside,' she called out, and she ran up the church path.

'That girl!' said Mrs Carter.

'Give her the ball and she'll run with it,' her husband agreed.

Mrs Carter nodded. 'I was saying as much to myself this morning.'

'Bloody marvellous!'

'I suppose so,' said Mrs Carter, and she gave him a wistful smile. She recognised in Annie all the eagerness and energy she had once possessed before time's tide had sucked it out of her.

Annie was unimpressed with the angels.

There were no fewer than twenty-two of them, two teams of eleven facing each other across the roof. Yes, they were all wearing lovely flowing cream gowns, and their collars and hems were braided with different colours, but the trouble is, thought Annie, they all look like they were painted yesterday.

They're so tight-lipped, she thought. Trying to squeeze out sour little smiles. And their eyes! I can see they're blue, but they're expressionless. Like marbles.

Mr Carter swung in on his sticks, grasped the carved poppy pew-end, and levered himself into the nearest seat.

'You all right, Dad?' his wife asked.

'Not today,' he said. 'Let's have a look at the pamphlet, then.'

'That costs.'

'I'll put it back after.'

Sandy and Dad, thought Annie. They're as bad as each other.

Mrs Carter padded up the nave alongside Annie. 'Found what you want, then?'

'I don't know what I'm looking for,' Annie replied.

Her mother stared up at the roof and frowned.

'I will, though.'

'There's angels all over the shop,' Mr Carter called out.

'Dad!' said Mrs Carter. 'Keep your voice down.'

'The ones in the roof, and more in the stained glass.'

'Over there, see!' said Annie. 'They look like they're throwing something. Hammmer-throwers! They can't be.'

'And more up on the stone seats beside the altar,' Mr Carter encouraged her.

Annie hurried up to the east end of the church.

'These ones look like they're swimming breaststroke,' Annie told her mother. 'Well, learning to. Look at them, straining their necks, trying to keep their heads above water.'

'Novices,' Mrs Carter agreed.

'What's that?'

'I don't know. Apprentices. Learners. You and your imagination.'

'Hey!' Mr Carter called out, waving the pamphlet, and Annie and his wife walked sedately back towards him.

'Calling out like that!' Mrs Carter said mildly. 'You've no respect for God's house.'

'I have,' said Mr Carter. 'What it says is these angels, the ones in the roof, were peppered with musket-shot . . .'

'What-a-what?' asked Annie.

'Bullets! A musket's an old gun.'

Annie narrowed her eyes and nodded. The same as Smasher's men, she thought. 'Shoot at them. Pepper them. Puncture them like colanders.'

'But somehow,' Mr Carter read, 'they escaped the fate of the angels in the church at Waterslain.'

'Whatever that was,' Annie said.

'I can't see any bullet-holes,' Mrs Carter said.

'No,' replied Mr Carter. 'They've all been painted over.'

'They don't look real,' Annie complained. 'Not like our wing, all marsh-green and yellowy-orange and vermilion. That's real.'

'It is,' Mr Carter agreed.

'Who exactly shot at these angels, anyhow?' Annie asked.

Mr Carter consulted the pamphlet again. 'It doesn't say,' he replied.

'It's something to do with the Ref . . . the Ref . . .' said Annie. 'I can't remember. Or Oliver Cromwell. That's what our rector wrote—you know, in the village hall.'

Mr Carter frowned slightly and then began to warble:

> *'Oliver Cromwell lay buried and dead.*
> *Hee-haw, buried and dead.'*

'Dad!' said Annie, a bit shocked.

> *'There grew an old apple-tree over his head*
> *Hee-haw, over his head.'*

'No respect!' Mrs Carter murmured.

> *'And he made an old woman go hippety-hop,*
> *Hee-haw, hippety-hop.'*

Mr Carter grinned, 'and that's all I know about Oliver Cromwell.'

'Who was he, anyhow?' Annie asked. 'Oliver Cromwell.'

'Lord Protector of England,' said her father. 'He came from Huntingdon or thereabouts. You'll have to ask Miss McQueen about him, Annie.'

'Not in the holidays,' Annie replied.

'She's not just your old schoolteacher, you

know. She's written a booklet about Waterslain.'

'I know,' said Annie in a cross voice, kicking at the tiles with one toe of her sensible sandals.

'And you could ask her to play you that song while you're about it.'

'Dad!' objected Annie.

On their way home, all at 29mph, Annie felt rather discontented. The trouble is, she thought, I'm searching without knowing where to look at all. I know each clue could be crucial, but everything seems like it could be a clue.

First they met an AA man in his yellow van and he saluted them, and then a black Ford Consul overtook the Carters' car.

'The Reverend,' said Mrs Carter. 'And Mrs Potter.'

'In a devil of a hurry,' Mr Carter added.

'Our Imp's just . . . an Imp,' Annie said. 'A piece of mischief. But devils, they've got black business.'

'I didn't say the Reverend was a devil,' Mr Carter replied.

'I know,' said Annie.

'Whatever do you mean?' asked Mrs Carter. 'Black business. Where did that come from?'

Annie didn't reply. She didn't know exactly. But she could see Pitterpatter shaking his head and hear him saying, 'The Black Book's locked in the vestry chest. One day, maybe, Annie.'

That's it, she thought. That's the next stone in the field. The Black Book. The old church accounts. I've got to see exactly what they say.

'Slow down, Tom!' Mrs Carter said. 'Right down! There, Annie! That's yarroway. Like cow parsley.'

Annie looked at the long-stalked flowers on the

36

verge of the lane, the throng of angel-flowers swaying in and out of sunlight. Each pinkish flower was winking at her.

5

Annie was up in the hammerbeam roof again, standing on the top rung of an extending ladder, surrounded by a spray of smiling angels. It was all cobwebby and she was wearing her best blouse.

In the round tower, the bell was tolling. Its pulse was steady as a heartbeat. It sounds so old, thought Annie. I know it's up above me but it's all around me. And somehow it's deep down, like something I've forgotten.

Each time the bell swung and the tongue struck the rim, all the angels trembled and Annie's ladder shook.

When she looked down, Annie saw at once that she was wearing Wellington boots. Two left-footed boots. That's strange, she thought. I don't remember putting them on. I didn't know I had two left feet.

Then Annie saw all her angels were wearing Wellingtons as well, left-footed ones with the bottoms of their creamy linen shifts neatly tucked into them.

No, not Wellingtons, thought Annie. Thigh-boots. Waders. The same as Billie and Laddie wear because they're in and out of the creek all the time, rinsing sacks of cockles and mussels, helping people on and off the little ferry. I've never seen them not wearing waders. I wouldn't be surprised if they wore them to bed.

At this moment, the angels around Annie began to whistle warnings. At first the sound was all on one note, then it began to rise, jerky and broken.

Then Annie heard a sound below her, and as soon as she peered down, she saw them. The whisperers. The dark whisperers. Smasher's men. Bullies and bruisers and crooks.

At once the whisperers began to raise their voices even though they were in church. They started to call out.

'Look at that one.'

'On the ladder.'

'She's moving.'

'She's real. She is.'

'Real eyes.'

'Come on, angel. Angel-flower!'

Then all Smasher's men jostled round the bottom of the ladder, and the ladder shuddered, and Annie thought she was going to fall over sideways.

The angels in the roof whistled their warnings more loudly.

'We'll get you,' yelled one voice.

'Gut you.'

'Hack you.'

'We'll have you.'

'That one will bleed real blood.'

'No!' cried Annie. 'No! I'm no angel.'

But Smasher's men were making such a clamour they couldn't hear her.

'I'm not!' yelled Annie. 'You ask my mother.'

'A real angel,' bellowed a voice below her, and its owner was scaling the ladder.

'I'm not!' cried Annie. 'I haven't even got wings.'

In the body of the church, an organ began to play. High notes, like the whistling and piping angels. Gruff low notes, hoots, guffaws, like

39

Smasher's men. Annie's protests, her cries. The rough music grew louder, louder until it seemed to Annie she was no longer standing on the top rung of the ladder, but drowning in sound, swirling and falling and drowning.

6

'When was I born?' Annie asked her mother.

'Teatime.'

'No, I mean, what day?'

'Tuesday. Tuesday's child is full of grace.'

'Angels are full of grace,' said Annie.

'Not angels again,' Mrs Carter replied.

'What's a blue angel?' Annie asked her.

'I've no idea. What is it?'

Annie grinned. 'I don't know. I made it up. I'm going out. Hippety-hopping.'

'No, you're not, young lady. We're driving into Fakenham.'

'How is it,' demanded Annie, 'that when I want us to drive out, you say we've got to stay in, and when I want to stay round here, we have to drive out?'

'Because!' said her mother. 'You're forgetting your dad has a haircut on Wednesday mornings— well, each fortnight. And I'm going to market. You can give me a hand with all the veg, and I've got to get more Beecham's. And remind me about the Lucozade.'

'And then I'm going to Baker's,' Annie told her.

'Whatever for?'

'Don't know,' said Annie. She waved her right forefinger and mimicked her mother's voice. 'You just don't know, Annie. You never can tell.'

Mrs Carter laughed. 'Get away with you,' she said.

What Annie unearthed in Baker's Antiques was Alan Leppard, the garage mechanic. He was in the upper room, the long, dusty silent one, and the moment Annie saw him, she realised she had seen him in her dream the night before. He was the whisperer who called her 'angel-flower', and started to climb the ladder after her. He was one of Smasher's men.

Annie curled up her toes. She took a step backward.

'Annie! You all right then?'

Annie nodded. 'You?' she mouthed.

'Found anything?'

'Um! Nothing.'

'Where's your mum, then?'

'In the market. Dad's having a haircut.'

Alan's dark eyes flashed and he ran his fingers through his dark, greasy mane. 'He hasn't got none.'

'He has,' objected Annie.

'None to speak of,' said Alan, grinning. 'No offence, mind. Pauline's in the market, too. And the brats. We've all come in.'

'What's in that bag, then?' asked Annie.

Alan fished into his dirty white canvas bag and pulled out a little clay figurine. A boy bare as the day he was born, with chubby pink cheeks. His arms were half-raised and he seemed to be dancing on air.

'Oh, he's lovely!' exclaimed Annie.

Alan tenderly stroked the boy's curly fair hair with his big, blunt right forefinger. 'A little angel,' he said.

'Are you buying him?' asked Annie.

'Buying?' answered the garage man. 'Selling more like.'

'Selling! Whose is he?'

'Mine,' replied Leppard curtly.

'No, I mean, where did you get him? Where does he come from?'

'None of your business, darling.'

'Well . . . what does he cost?'

Alan Leppard tapped the end of his nose. 'More than you've got,' he said, smiling. 'Oh yes!'

'You will sell him to someone who'll really look after him, won't you?' asked Annie.

The garage man shrugged. 'So long as I get the right price.'

'Can I hold him?'

Alan laid the innocent little angel between Annie's hands and, cradling and nursing him, Annie remembered her mother telling her how Alan had stolen the lead from Waterslain church roof, at least that's what everyone suspected, though no one could prove it.

'Not just that,' Mrs Carter had said. 'Those wooden saints in Wycherley church. Poor little blighters. Who nicked them if that wasn't Alan? He's been sent down, you know.'

'Where?'

'Sent down. To prison. Him and his mates robbed a post office, and Alan went to prison for three years. He's a charmer, all right, but as light-fingered as they come. Leopards never change their spots!'

'Mum!'

'That's why the Reverend Potter is giving him odd jobs,' her mother went on. 'Trying to teach him to earn a living. You know: keeping him on the straight and narrow.'

'Pitterpatter told me Alan was on the point of taking the angel's wing to the dump,' said Annie, 'and it was a good thing he went up to the attic when he did.'

Mrs Carter pursed her lips. 'A likely story!' she said. 'No, you can't trust Alan further than you can throw him.'

No one was going to throw Alan anywhere in a hurry. He was so big. So hairy. So sweaty.

Annie gave the little angel boy back to him.

'Saw you in the hall. Sizing up that wing.'

'Oh!' exclaimed Annie. 'It's so beautiful. So real.'

'And you went round Creake.'

'How do you know?' asked Annie, startled.

The garage man looked at Annie thoughtfully. His dark eyes were sharp as tacks.

'How do you know?' she asked again.

'The Reverend's wife told me. She saw your Imp.'

Annie felt a bit breathless.

'Them angels are around somewhere,' said Alan. 'Bound to be.'

'Do you think so?' asked Annie.

'Stands to reason.' Leppard narrowed his eyes at Annie again. 'Don't it, angel-flower?'

Annie stared at him, alarmed. Her mouth went dry and she kept swallowing. 'I've got to go,' she said. 'Mum will be waiting.'

'Right,' said the garage-man. 'Well, if you do find out anything, you come and tell Alan.'

Annie almost ran out of Baker's and across to the market. And there she saw her mother standing by a stall, talking to another woman. It was Gracie.

There was no sign of Sandy, though. He's always sort of invisible anyhow, thought Annie. Maybe he's made himself disappear altogether.

Annie walked up behind her mother and Gracie.

'Well,' Gracie was saying, 'to be honest, I'm no more pleased to see you than you are me.'

Mrs Carter snorted. 'What did you expect?'

'Margie, Margie . . .'

'Don't you Margie me!'

'Can't you forgive and forget?'

'Not until hell freezes over.'

'Mum!' ventured Annie nervously.

Mrs Carter swung round. 'Ah! Annie. Just in time.'

'Hello, Mrs Boroff,' Annie said.

'Gracie to you,' Gracie replied. 'Hi, Annie!'

At this moment Sandy reappeared at his mother's side. 'Hi, Annie,' he said.

'You all right?' said Annie. And then, before you could say Jack Robinson, 'Come and look at this!'

Annie darted round the stall's canvas flap and Sandy drifted after her. 'They're arguing,' she said.

'What about?'

'Don't know. It doesn't matter. We've got to talk.'

'You look like you've seen a ghost,' said Sandy.

'Can we meet later?'

'In the church.'

'Straight after dinner.'

'Dinner!' Sandy exclaimed. He blew out his pale cheeks and peered through his goggles. 'Mom wouldn't let me—not that late.'

'That's not late!' exclaimed Annie.

'Oh!' said Sandy. 'You mean lunch. Okey-dokey.'

'Dinner,' said Annie. 'See you then.'

7

Annie reached the church first. At least she was pretty sure she did. 'Sandy?' she called out in a cautious voice as soon as she stepped in; and then, much more loudly, 'Sandy!'

Annie climbed the steps to the pulpit, just to make sure. And while she was up there, she arched her back and gazed at the roof. All her angels had disappeared again, their waders and wings and whistling, everything.

Where are you, she breathed. Tell me. Please tell me.

Annie was interrupted from her reverie by—what? A shift of light. She looked down the nave. A figure was standing in a dazzling sunshaft.

Annie blinked. 'Sandy? It is you, isn't it?'

'No,' said Sandy.

'I couldn't see your face. The sun's dazzling me.'

'I dazzled you,' said Sandy.

'Where have you been?'

'Inside a pillar.'

'Of sunlight.'

'No,' replied Sandy. 'Come and look,'

Annie scrambled down from the pulpit and followed Sandy to the back of the church.

'This stone pillar or column or whatever it is,' said Sandy. 'You can step right inside it.'

'Let me try,' said Annie. And then: 'It's colder than inside a tree trunk. And drier. Not so creepy-crawly.' Annie stepped out of the pillar again.

'Some people get buried standing up,' observed Sandy.

'They don't.'

'It was in Readers' Digest.'

'Really? But you don't think . . .'

'No,' interrupted Sandy.

'Why not?'

'It's impossible. This pillar was built hundreds of years before the angels were in danger.'

'Before they were fledglings,' Annie said. 'Before they saw battle-lights.'

Sandy blinked. 'Well remembered,' he said.

Then Annie told Sandy about how she'd met Alan Leppard in Baker's, and how he was selling a little clay angel. She told him about her mother believing Alan had stolen the wooden saints from Wycherley church, and how he'd been in prison for three years.

'Wow!' exclaimed Sandy.

'And Alan said the Waterslain angels are bound to be around somewhere.'

'He did?'

'And he wanted me to tell him if I find out anything.'

'Sure!'

'He's searching for them himself,' said Annie, 'and he's keeping a watch on us. He scares me.'

'Yeah,' agreed Sandy.

'He even knew I'd been to Creake church,' Annie said. 'I went with Mum and Dad to see their angels. And, yesterday, I listed all the flowers with angel-names: Angel's Trumpets and Angel's Eyes and Archangels and Angel's Pincushions, and I can't remember. And . . .' Annie nearly told Sandy about her terrifying dream, and how Alan was in it, but then she realised she didn't want to share absolutely everything. '. . . well, lots of other

47

things,' she ended lamely.

Sandy smiled a watery smile. 'Lots of other things you're not going to tell me about,' he said. He swung round the carved poppy pew-end, sat down and shuffled sideways to make room for Annie. 'I walked up to the staithe.'

'Down,' said Annie. 'Sea-level.'

'Down, then,' said Sandy. 'And I sat in a rowboat.'

'You've got a boat?'

'Nope,' said Sandy. 'And I just looked at the sunlight on the water. Ribs. Wings. Angels dancing in the water.'

'Dancing,' asked Annie, 'or drowning? I've seen angels between clouds sometimes, opening and shutting their blue wings. Now you see them, now you don't.'

'That's probably how real angels are,' Sandy said. 'Whatever real is.'

'Sky-angels,' Annie went on, as much to herself as Sandy. 'Water-angels. Flower-angels . . .'

'Snow-angels,' added Sandy. 'At home, we make them each winter.'

'You're lucky.'

'You fall back into the snow, and flap your arms, and then get up very carefully.'

Annie smiled. She thought of her little nephew Storm, and how he'd do that, and yell, 'Again! Again!'

'You couldn't do that here,' said Annie. 'Well, not often. We don't have enough snow.'

'The thing is,' said Sandy, 'sky-angels and water-angels and flower-angels and snow-angels are all well and good, but where are they getting us?'

'You said we've got to consider each and every

clue.'

'At the moment we're like chickens, still running all over the place after their heads have been cut off.'

'We've got to beat Alan Leppard to it,' said Annie.

'We need more facts about our angels, the ones who used to be here,' Sandy went on. 'That note beside the wing in the hall said that in the Black Book in the church . . .'

'I know,' said Annie. 'I asked Pitterpatter if I could see it and he said no.'

'Why not?' demanded Sandy.

'Actually,' Annie said, 'I do know where it is.'

Annie had never stepped beyond the blotchy old green baize curtain into the little vestry. It was like a secret room, a quite ordinary room really, with a high, cobwebby leaded window, and Pitterpatter's cassock and surplice hanging on two pegs on the wall, and a table covered by a floral tablecloth with a bar of Lifebuoy soap and one long grey sock and a bottle of lemonade and two Dinky toys on it, one a car saying Brooke Bond Tea, and the other . . .

'A Delta Wing!' exclaimed Sandy. 'A Gloster Javelin. I made one from balsa wood, but it was too big to bring with us.'

A quite ordinary room except that in one corner stood a large oak chest, sturdy and cracked and quietly gleaming.

Sandy advanced on the chest, gripped the lip of the heavy lid with both hands, and tried to lift it.

It was locked.

Annie delved into her left pocket and pulled out her penknife.

'Cool!' said Sandy.

49

'It won't work, probably,' Annie said. 'It's not a spring. It's a deadlock.'

'What's that?'

Annie poked and prodded the lock with her penknife. 'No,' she said. 'We need the key.'

'A huge one by the look of it,' Sandy replied. 'At least the minister won't be carrying it around on his key-ring.' He started searching along the dirty skirting-boards. Under the bottle of lemonade. In the inside pocket of Pitterpatter's cassock. And then, up on a chair, on the high window-ledge.

'Got it!' Sandy exclaimed triumphantly.

'Wow! I'll do it.'

Annie inserted the key into the lock but then she paused. 'They could be in here.'

Sandy shook his head. 'They wouldn't fit in,' he said.

'Parts of them.'

'The minister's not hiding them,' Sandy objected.

Annie turned the key in the lock. Then she and Sandy heaved up the lid and tipped it back against the wall. And there, on a velvet cushion, lay the Black Book. Without a word, Annie reverently lifted it, and Sandy made room for it on the table.

'Careful!' breathed Annie. 'The cover's crumbly. Wow! The pages are all stiff.'

To begin with, Annie and Sandy couldn't make head or tail of the spindly black script. And then Annie heard a rustling in one corner of the vestry, and saw a real tail.

'What was it?' Sandy asked nervously.

'Only a harvest mouse. There's millions around.'

'Whew!'

'Them and coypu.'

'What?'

'In the marsh. I'll tell you later.'

'What if the minister shows up?' asked Sandy.

Annie shook her head and sighed. 'We'll just have to . . . I don't know. Let's pray he doesn't.'

After a while, Annie and Sandy began to pick out characters and then words. Then whole phrases. They turned the stiff pages. *Payd for destroying . . . destroying of 12 Jackdaws . . . Payd Gam Gregory for 2 days and 1/2 work spreading the mould in the churchyard . . . Payd to Arthur Andrews for curing the chaplain's cow . . .*

Pd John Docking for the bell ringing and grave making . . .

Register: Oliver Mousey was buried in an erect position at his own request . . .

Sandy elbowed Annie. 'I told you,' he said.

'Look!' said Annie, her voice trembling. 'Look!'

July 1455 Pd to John Chisel for carving 14 angels and erecting in roof . . . 2 shillings.

Annie and Sandy stared at the words.

'I never touched anything this old,' said Sandy. 'Son of a gun! Columbus hadn't even discovered America by then.'

'It sounds so, well, normal,' said Annie. 'So everyday.'

'Yeah,' agreed Sandy. 'Like the next item on a shopping-list. How much is two shillings?'

'Um!' said Annie. 'Nine bags of crisps. Almost ten.'

'You're joking.'

'It was more then. In 1455.'

'Must have been,' agreed Sandy. 'Much, much

51

more. What's that in the margin?'

Annie screwed up her eyes. 'It's so small. Like a fly wrote it with one leg. Something . . . something. Angels, is it?'

Sandy shook his head. 'I can't do writing that small.'

Annie clicked her tongue. 'Angels Waterslain.'

'We know that already,' said Sandy.

'It's just a sort of heading,' said Annie. 'It's not the same handwriting, I don't think it is.' She clicked her tongue. 'We're not getting anywhere. We're just not looking in the right place.'

'You don't know that,' Sandy said. 'Maybe we are. But maybe we're not looking in the right kind of way. I mean, a few secs ago, we couldn't read this writing, and now we can, because we've learned how to look at it.'

'I see what you mean,' said Annie. 'The note in the church hall said descendants of the man who made the angels . . .'

'John Chisel,' said Sandy.

'It said some of them still live in Norfolk. I ought to go and see them.'

'Are we in this together?' Sandy demanded.

'Yes! Yes, we are,' Annie corrected herself. 'I mean both of us,'

'My mom will drive us if it's a long way,' volunteered Sandy. 'The day after tomorrow we gotta go and stay with my cousins. Near Lincoln.'

'How long for?' asked Annie.

'I dunno, two nights I think, but after that, she will.'

'And before that,' offered Annie, 'I'll show you the marsh if you want.'

Sandy looked rather doubtful. 'Do I?'

'It's my secret place,' Annie told him. 'I'll show you tomorrow.'

'OK,' said Sandy. 'And I'll ask Mom if she knows any Chisels. She knows everyone.'

8

'Owk!' yelled Sandy.

He tried to pull his left leg out of the mud-hole. The mud sucked and slurped and would not let it go. Then Sandy clasped both hands behind his thigh, but that made him lose his balance, and he sat down in the squelch.

Annie laughed. 'You walked straight into it. Your marsh christening.'

'I do not love this place,' Sandy said.

'It's the best,' cried Annie. 'The only place.'

When Sandy tried to stand up again, his left leg sank into the mud-hole almost up to his hip. As high as a wader.

'Come on,' said Annie. 'Give me your hands.' Then she pulled him backwards until the mud-hole did let go of Sandy's foot and splattered them both with dark spots.

'It's good for you,' grinned Annie.

'What is?'

'Mud. The iodine in it. Mum says so.'

Sandy inspected himself and wiped his arms and legs with a handful of couch-grass.

'That won't get it off,' said Annie. 'Wait until Dead Man's Pool.'

'Where?'

'You can wash it off there. Oh, no! Look who's coming.'

'Hello there!' called the Reverend Potter, loud and cheerful as always. 'Annie and . . . um . . .'

'Sandy,' Annie told him. 'What's that pole for?'

'Sandy, yes. I've heard about you.' The

54

Reverend Potter waved a long hooked pole in the air. 'Oh!' he said. 'Prodding around. You know.'

'It looks like what pirates use,' said Sandy, 'for snagging and boarding.'

'Sandy stepped into the mud-hole,' Annie explained.

'So I see.'

Sandy flapped his arms in a helpless way, then left them sticking out like a cormorant hanging out its black wings to dry.

The Reverend Potter laughed. 'A sort of marsh angel,' he observed.

'Angels haven't got black wings,' said Annie.

'Evil ones have,' Pitterpatter replied. 'Satan, for instance. He's a dark angel.'

'Do they wear black Wellingtons?' Annie asked. 'You know, or waders?'

'Have they got black spots all over them?' added Sandy.

The rector smiled. 'I wouldn't know. Are you two walking up to Dead Man's Pool?'

Annie and Sandy and the Reverend Potter fell into step, and the wiry marsh grass rasped as they brushed their way through it.

'Can I ask you a question?' Annie began.

'Fire away!' said Pitterpatter.

'You know that wing? In the hall?'

'I certainly do,' Pitterpatter replied.

'I mean,' Annie went on, 'Sandy and I know about angel height and angel flowers and snow-angels and that, but what is an angel, exactly?'

The Reverend Potter strode on to a rickety walkway over one of the wider creeks—just a plank with a shaky old handrail on either side.

55

Under his weight, it bounced. Then he put down the long, hooked pole, turned round and faced Annie and Sandy.

Oh, thought Annie. He doesn't know about the chest and the Black Book, does he? Has he found out?

'What is an angel, exactly?' the rector repeated. 'Easy to ask, but difficult to answer. Or rather, there are lots of answers.'

'What's yours?' asked Sandy.

'I believe angels are superhuman. They may look like us . . .'

'Except they've got wings,' said Annie.

'And they need those wings to fly between heaven and earth, carrying God's messages. That's their work.'

'Like Gabriel,' said Sandy.

'Like Gabriel,' Pitterpatter agreed. 'He announced God's plan to Mary. Angels announce and they comfort us, sometimes they warn. I think myself that they're invisible but can appear like humans when they want to.'

'Do they need to eat and sleep and, well, go to the bog and everything?' asked Annie.

Pitterpatter smiled. 'I honestly don't know. I don't suppose so. Muslims believe angels are made out of light. I rather like that.'

'And they're very beautiful,' Annie added.

'Yes, but not like gorgeous film stars. And the male ones aren't rugged or beefy. They look more . . . more holy than humans do.'

Sandy blinked at the Reverend Potter through his owl-glasses.

'There's part of each of us,' said the rector, 'an inner part, that knows what's good and right and

56

true. A part that never needs to ask.'

'You just know,' said Sandy.

'Indeed,' said Pitterpatter. 'Heaven knows, I'm no angel. But I'm sure that part is the angel in each of us.'

'But how can you see them?' Annie demanded. 'And where do they come from? And are you only an angel after you die, or can a living person become an angel?'

'Questions, questions,' said Pitterpatter, smiling. 'I don't know the answers. What I know is we must all search for our own angels.'

'You mean the part inside us?' Sandy enquired.

'Or our Waterslain angels?' added Annie.

'Ah,' said Pitterpatter, and he gave Annie a knowing look. 'Well, I think we're all doing that, aren't we?'

'Both, then,' said Sandy. 'Can the angel part of us talk to real angels?'

'Well,' said Pitterpatter, 'all things are possible . . .'

'Do they want us to find them?' asked Annie. 'And can we ask them for their help?'

Pitterpatter shrugged. 'Many hymns tell us so.' He stooped and picked up his pole. 'Now, then. Dead Man's Pool?'

9

'No,' Gracie Boroff told Sandy. 'I can't say I've ever heard the name.'

'Chisel,' Sandy tried again.

'Chesney . . . yes,' mused Gracie. 'Chivers . . . Chubb . . . No, I haven't.'

But Annie had better luck.

'Chisel,' said her father. 'Haven't heard that name in ages.'

'Why do you want to know?' her mother asked.

'John Chisel carved the missing angels.'

'Oh! So that's it,' Margie Carter exclaimed. 'Hundreds of years ago, he did.'

'The Chisels emigrated to Australia,' Annie's father said. 'But the boy came back to college here. Years ago. I'm blessed if I can remember his name. This stroke's taken off half my memory.'

'That was Loafer,' said Annie's mother. 'Least, that's what everyone called him. We were in the same class before he went away. His real name was Sariel.'

'Sariel, yes,' said Mr Carter.

'What kind of name is that?' asked Annie.

'The Lord knows,' Mr Carter replied.

'Yes, Loafer went to college and he lived with his mum's older sister in Diss,' Mrs Carter told Annie, 'Josie Sidebottom, yes. She was a Waterslain girl.'

'Until he married?' asked Annie.

'He never did,' her mother said. 'Not that I heard. I heard he was very poorly.'

'That's sorted, then,' said Mr Carter.

'I've got to talk to him,' Annie announced. 'Sariel Chisel.'

'Whatever for?' her mother asked, startled.

'My angel quest.'

'Whatever's got into the girl?' Mrs Carter asked, without really expecting an answer. She knew how Annie got these bees in her bonnet and was thankful for them. 'If there's one thing I can't stand,' she often said, 'it's hearing children say they're bored.'

'Would I be able to ring Loafer up?' Annie asked.

'Don't you call him that, girl,' her mother said.

'Mr Chisel, then.'

'I don't suppose he's still living with his aunt,' Mrs Carter replied. 'Not after all these years.' She turned to her husband. 'That'll cost, a call to Diss. What do you say, Tom?'

Mr Carter sucked his cheeks. 'You'll have to ask the operator for a number. That'll be a number for Mrs Sidebottom.'

'Thanks, Dad.'

'You give it a try, girl.'

The operator found a number for Mrs Josie Sidebottom. Diss 2375.

'Diss,' said Mr Carter. 'Foreigners! Fifty miles, must be. Go on, then. Give it a try, girl.'

When the operator put Annie through, a woman answered the phone. She sounded old.

'Can I please speak to Mr Chisel?' Annie asked politely. 'Um . . . Mr Sariel Chisel.'

'Who's that speaking?'

'Annie Carter. From Waterslain.'

'I'm sorry, dear.'

Annie frowned. 'I can ring later if you want.'

59

'No, dear. No.' There was an awkward pause. 'Mr Chisel died on Tuesday.'

Annie gasped.

'You weren't to know, dear.'

'No, I didn't.'

'No, of course not.'

'I'm so sorry. I mean, I'm sorry to bother you.'

'Thank you, dear.'

Annie didn't know what else to say. 'Well . . .' she said haltingly, 'goodbye, then.'

'What was all that about?' Mrs Carter asked.

'Mr Chisel died on Tuesday,' Annie told her parents.

'Blast!' Mr Carter said under his breath. 'He wasn't that old.'

'Same age as me,' Mrs Carter said.

'She didn't say why or anything?'

Annie shook her head.

'Well, you'll have to wait until after the funeral,' her mother told Annie. 'Maybe Josie Sidebottom can help you.'

'I know,' said Annie slowly, and then her face began to light up. 'You told me Miss McQueen has written a book about Waterslain.'

'Yes, well, a little booklet,' her father replied.

'And she knows about Cromwell.'

'Probably.'

'My goodness!' said Mrs Carter. 'You really are all abuzz!'

'Mum!'

'You can ask her about it after your next piano lesson.'

'No,' said Annie. 'I'm going to see her now. Hippety-hop.'

'Wait a minute, young lady,' Mrs Carter said.

'You can take round some of this samphire. It's well rinsed.'

Miss McQueen lived up Gong Lane, and she was out in her neat little garden, correcting wilful plants, trimming wayward offshoots with her secateurs, and lightly pinching her unripe greengages. She looked at her visitor over her half-glasses.

'Annie!' she exclaimed, with a quizzical little smile.

Annie proffered the bunch of virulent green samphire, now slightly warm and slightly sticky. 'From Mum. I picked it.'

'How very nice. Thank you, dear.'

'Please can I ask you some questions?' asked Annie, in a serious voice. 'I mean, is it all right in the holidays?'

Light and rapid as a butterfly, a look of pleasure flickered across Miss McQueen's face. 'I was just about to make a cup of tea. Would you like to have some?'

'All right,' said Annie. 'Is it true Admiral Nelson used to walk down here? When he was a boy?'

'If he was making a beeline from Burnham Thorpe to the creek and the staithe,' Miss McQueen replied, 'this was the way he came. Straight past my front door.'

'Dear Waterslain,' said Annie. 'The holy view.'

Miss McQueen smiled. 'Ah, yes. That verse in the village hall.'

'Who wrote it?' asked Annie.

'My father.'

'Really?'

Miss McQueen nodded.

'Why didn't it say so, under the poem?'

'Oh! I thought anyone who really wanted to find out would easily be able to.'

'It's lovely,' said Annie. 'I've seen the island looking like it said. All golden.'

'My father was pretending to be Admiral Nelson,' explained Miss McQueen, 'remembering when he was a boy in Waterslain. Now come in, dear. Just take off your shoes, if you don't mind.'

Somehow, thought Annie, her face is as unlined as a baby's—well, not a newborn baby, they're all wrinkled. Her skin's all pale and smooth, but her eyes are a bit faded.

Annie had never been inside Miss McQueen's cottage before. Each ornament was in its proper and precise place, and it was very still. The only sound was the gentle ticking of the slender grandmother clock in the hall. There was a scent, slight but unmistakable, of dried rose petals.

'Penny for your thoughts, Annie.'

'Oh! I'm sorry,' said Annie, shaking her head. 'It's like, well, I don't know how to say it exactly.'

'Say it, though,' Miss McQueen encouraged her.

'I know the clock's ticking, and it's lovely, but it's like time has stopped in here.'

'Yes,' said Miss McQueen. 'Well, I do try to leave time outside my front door. Now I'll just put the kettle on.'

While she was doing so, Annie tried to work out what to ask. What I want to find out, she thought, is everything she knows about our angels. But I don't want to tell her exactly why I'm asking.

'Have you heard of Smasher?' Annie began.

'Smasher?'

'Yes.'

'What do you mean? Smasher what?'

'I don't know.'

'Is it a person?'

'Yes.'

'Who is he?'

'I don't know.'

Miss McQueen's mouth tightened. 'Well, this isn't going to get us very far, is it?'

Annie tried another tack. 'You know the angels in South Creake?'

'Such a shame,' said Miss McQueen. 'They've had the life beaten out of them.'

'When they were shot at?'

'No. By the men who made such a botch of restoring them. They all look exactly the same, with their staring eyes and thin little smiles.'

'The pamphlet says they were peppered with musket shot.'

'That's right. It does.'

'Well, why?'

Miss McQueen nodded. What I've always liked, she thought, is how persistent Annie is. She just goes on nagging away at something until she's got the answer.

'Do you remember we learned about Henry the Eighth?'

'Yes,' said Annie in a cautious voice.

'Well, when he broke away from Rome . . . When he started the Church of England, he wanted to get rid of all the Roman Catholic ornaments in our churches. All the stained glass, and wall-paintings, and pictures of the Virgin Mary and the saints, like the ones on the rood-screen in Waterslain church.'

'They're half-wrecked,' said Annie.

'Exactly,' Miss McQueen agreed. 'And so are all

the statues and carvings and the tombstones. His men even pulled down crucifixes and crosses. The king thought that all these things cluttered up churches, and stopped people from thinking about God Himself.'

'So did he shoot the angels, then?'

Miss McQueen winced. 'Maybe, Annie, but it's not quite as simple as that. After Henry died, England became Roman Catholic again. The Church of England and the Roman Catholics struggled for almost one hundred years, and because of their faith, people on both sides were tortured. Some were burned alive.'

'That's horrible!' cried Annie.

'And Oliver Cromwell's men finished the job King Henry had started almost one hundred years before. They smoked King Charles' soldiers out of churches where they were taking sanctuary; they imprisoned them in churches, they even hanged and beheaded them in churches. So it may have been King Henry's men and it may have been Cromwell's men who peppered the Creake angels with musket-shot. They were wreckers. Destroyers! They gutted and hacked and punctured and ripped.' Miss McQueen's voice was trembling with indignation, and all at once she slapped her open palm against her forehead, and gave a little cry.

'Are you all right?' Annie asked anxiously.

'How could I have forgotten! Smasher! You mean Smasher Dowsing.'

'Who?'

'William Dowsing was Cromwell's Commissioner for the Destruction of . . . I can't remember exactly. Yes, Iconoclast General! That's

64

what he was called. Iconoclast General. Anyhow, he wrecked many East Anglian churches. He hated angels more than anything. Cherubim, he called them.' Miss McQueen frowned. 'Who told you about William Dowsing, Annie?'

'He came to Waterslain,' Annie replied.

Miss McQueen looked at Annie over her half-glasses.

'I know he did. I've seen him.'

'Seen him?' exclaimed her teacher.

'And all his men.'

'When, Annie?'

'Twice,' said Annie in a matter-of-fact voice. And then, before Miss McQueen could ask her any more awkward questions, 'What happened to our angels? Our Waterslain angels?'

Miss McQueen blinked.

'I mean, were they destroyed or did they escape?'

'Escape?'

'I don't mean fly away. I mean, did someone save them?'

Miss McQueen shook her head. 'Dowsing was very thorough,' she said. 'There's not much in our church that wasn't gouged, or whacked with a sledgehammer, or even worse. Maybe he really did come here to Waterslain.'

'But what if someone knew Smasher's men were coming, and rescued the angels,' Annie persisted. 'And if they were rescued, where do you think they were hidden?'

Miss McQueen smiled. 'You have to imagine,' she said. 'First you have to find out all you possibly can, and then you have to imagine. You have to become the people living in Cromwell's time,

65

worshipping each Sunday in our church. You have to become Smasher's men. You even have to become one of the angels.'

'Sometimes,' Annie said in an earnest voice, 'I do imagine I'm one of them. Up in the roof. And sometimes I think they'll show me where they are.'

'Imagine with your whole mind and heart,' Miss McQueen told Annie, 'and your imagining will guide you.'

10

On the afternoon that Sandy and Grace came back to Waterslain after staying with relatives, Annie rang Diss 2375 again, and the same old woman answered the telephone.

'I'm sorry to bother you again. It's Annie Carter from Waterslain.'

'Yes, dear. I did think I recognised you.'

'I'm so sorry about Mr Chisel.'

'Thank you, dear.'

'What I wonder is, well, are you Mrs Sidebottom?'

'Who's wanting to talk to her, then?' asked the voice at the other end of the line.

'Me,' said Annie.

'You are,' said the voice.

'I am what?'

'Talking to her.'

'Oh!' exclaimed Annie, suddenly feeling quite breathless. 'I think you know my mum. Least, Mr Chisel did. They were in the same class before he went to Australia.'

'Name of?' asked the voice.

'Margie. I mean, Margaret. Margaret Carter. No, she was Margaret Manning then.'

'No,' said the voice. 'I can't say I do.'

'Can I come and see you?' Annie asked. 'It's for, well, a holiday thing.'

'For what, dear?'

'A sort of quest. It's quite important. It won't take long.'

There was a silence at the other end of the line.

'It's a long way.'

'I know,' said Annie. 'Will the day after tomorrow be all right?'

'Whenever you like, dear. I don't get many visitors.'

Mrs Carter was quite put out when Annie reported that Gracie had already agreed to drive her and Sandy over.

'What's wrong with your dad?' she grumbled.

'Nothing,' retorted Annie in a cross voice.

'Don't you answer me back, madam.'

'I just didn't want to tire him out.'

'Hasn't that woman got anything better to do?'

'Mum!'

'She needs a job. Keep her out of mischief.'

On their way to Diss, Annie sat in the front with Gracie, and she found out plenty more about Bruce Boroff and the other handsome American G.I.s.

'It was a lovely May evening, and there was a dance in the village hall,' Gracie began.

'In Waterslain?' asked Annie.

'1943. I was wearing my red dress and dancing with Ken—we all called him the Spider because his arms and legs were so long and he was so hairy, and he used to sort-of creep around. Then in through the door swaggered these three gorgeous men.' Gracie took both hands off the driving wheel to illustrate just how smart and manly they were.

In the back of the car, Sandy sighed. If he'd heard this story once, he'd heard it one hundred times.

'Brilliantine. Big smiles. And their teeth were lovely—so white.'

'Didn't the Spider mind?' Annie asked.

'Too bad!' Gracie replied. 'Every girl in the hall kept looking at these guys, and one of them caught my eye, and as soon as my dance with Ken was done, he came straight over and asked for a dance.' Gracie gave a luxurious deep sigh. 'Glenn Miller it was,' she said. 'Moonlight Serenade.'

'A band? Really?'

Gracie smiled and shook her head. 'No! A record.'

'And that man,' asked Annie, 'was that Sandy's dad?'

Gracie turned and looked at Annie and opened her eyes wide.

'Oh!' breathed Annie.

'We didn't know where they came from, but we soon found out they were stationed at Sculthorpe. The runways had just been completed. Before that, they'd been at Raynham. On our first date, Bruce told me about Fireball. That was the first American bomber to fly into Raynham—dragging a man behind it after his parachute got caught. You must have heard about it.'

'Hundreds of times,' said a resigned voice in the back of the car.

'And Bruce was turret-gunner in the second bomber into Raynham,' Gracie went on. 'That was a B-17 too, Hell's Angel, and it was punctured all over. The hole in one wing was so large you could crawl through it. Oh, Annie! After that dance, life was never the same in Waterslain again.' Gracie was speaking louder and louder. 'In came the G.I.s with cigarettes and chocolate and perfume. Stockings! Real red-blooded men.'

Mum wouldn't talk about men like this, thought Annie. She'd say it was vulgar.

69

'Talking of chocolate,' said Gracie, reaching into the pocket of the car door, 'do you want a Rolo?'

'Please,' said Annie.

Gracie handed her the packet. 'Two each.'

'They're not as good as Hershey's Kisses,' Sandy said.

Gracie glanced to her right. 'There's the lane to Sculthorpe,' she said. 'You're right, Annie, it didn't half get up the noses of all the men. Just like it upset lots of women in the U.S. when the G.I.s brought home English brides. That's how it was, though.'

'All's fair in love and war,' said Annie. 'That's what Dad says.'

'I'm glad to hear it,' Gracie replied with some feeling. 'That I am. All's very sudden in love and war, that's for sure. I was swept off my feet. Before I knew it, I was promised to Bruce, and pregnant! Then he got stationed at Oulton and I had to take the bus over, and he brought me back in the truck.'

'Wow!' exclaimed Annie.

'Do you know, Annie, seventy thousand English girls became G.I. brides, and went to live in the U.S.? Seventy thousand! That's more than double the whole population of King's Lynn. We were called the Petticoat Pilgrims.'

'Did you like living in America?' asked Annie.

Gracie gave a small shrug. 'To begin with, I guess,' she replied. 'It all seemed so exciting to begin with.'

'I was a war baby,' Annie told her.

'And so's Sandy.' Gracie glanced in the rearview mirror. 'Sandy Dune Boroff.'

'Sandy Dune,' said Annie, grinning.

'Well, that's just a secret little joke between me and Brucie.'

For a while Annie sat tight, digesting all Gracie had told her. Then she twisted round in her seat, and Sandy gave her a Donald Duck look to say that he found his mother absolutely sickening.

11

'Josie Sidebottom?' asked Gracie.

The little white-haired woman looked up at her through her spectacles.

'I'm Gracie Boroff. With two children to meet you.'

'Two?' said Mrs Sidebottom.

'I brought a friend,' Annie explained. 'I hope you don't mind.'

'Come in, dear.'

'I won't myself,' said Gracie. 'I've got some shopping to do. They won't be a trouble to you.'

'Give us an hour, Mom,' Sandy said.

'All right, angel. Bye, then.' And with that, Gracie bounced away down the narrow path, bent down to rub the lavender, and turned to wave at the gate.

'Your mother?' Josie Sidebottom asked Annie.

'Oh no!' exclaimed Annie, quite taken aback. 'Sandy's.'

'Hi!' said Sandy, and stuck out his right hand.

'She sounds American,' said Mrs Sidebottom.

'Skin-deep,' said Sandy.

'So do you.'

'Actually,' explained Annie, 'Sandy's mum was born in Waterslain.'

'Now come in, both of you,' the old woman said. She shuffled across the hallway into the living room. 'We'll sit in here. There's not much room, I'm afraid. This whole flat's not much bigger than a postage-stamp.'

Sandy looked around and hung out his arms, in

72

the way he had done on the marsh. 'A big one,' he said. 'From the Vatican.'

'What, dear?'

'A big postage-stamp. From the Holy City. I collect stamps.'

'With Sariel here,' Mrs Sidebottom went on, 'we were packed in like sardines. There's more space for one.'

'Too much, I expect,' said Sandy, blinking behind his goggles.

'Thank you, dear. It does feel like that.'

'I'm very sorry about Mr Chisel,' Annie said. 'And my parents send their cond . . . cond . . .'

'Condolences,' said Sandy.

'Yes,' agreed Annie.

'Thank you, dear.' Mrs Sidebottom shook her head. 'It was a wicked illness. Went on for years, it did. Slow. Fierce.'

'I'm so sorry,' said Annie again. She didn't know what else to say.

'Sariel,' said Sandy. 'That's a strange name.'

'A family name,' Mrs Sidebottom replied. 'Lots of the men in the Chisel family were called by angel-names. Michael . . . Uriel . . . and then there was Raphael . . .'

'Sariel's an angel-name?' Sandy enquired, wrinkling up his forehead.

'Now just look after yourselves, will you?' Mrs Sidebottom told them. 'I'll be back in a jiffy.'

'We keep finding angels,' Sandy said quietly to Annie, 'but not the ones we're looking for.'

For a couple of minutes, Josie Sidebottom busied herself in the kitchen and then she shuffled back with two glasses of ginger beer and slices of fruit cake.

'Wow!' exclaimed Annie.

'Neato!' said Sandy.

'Well,' said Mrs Sidebottom. She smiled down at them, and her smile lit up her whole face. 'Why not?'

'You didn't have to,' said Annie.

The old woman sat herself down in her faded armchair beside the fireplace. Its arms were so high that she almost disappeared inside it. 'Don't wait to be asked,' she said. 'Help yourselves.'

Annie and Sandy fell on the cake like wolves. Then Annie offered a piece to Mrs Sidebottom.

'Well, perhaps I will,' she said. 'I shouldn't, mind.'

Mrs Sidebottom toyed with her cake and sort-of sucked at it, and Annie saw that most of it ended up in crumbs on her lap. Through her spectacles, the old woman stared at Annie and Sandy, patient and unblinking.

'We're doing a holiday quest,' Annie explained. 'We're trying to find the Waterslain angels.'

Mrs Sidebottom nodded. 'I did wonder,' she said. 'You're not the first.'

'No,' Sandy said. 'We're the last. We're going to be the last, Mrs Sidebottom.'

Mrs Sidebottom gave him a sharp look. 'You're a strange one, you are,' she said.

'If you don't mind my asking,' Annie said politely, 'before you married, was your surname Chisel?'

'No,' the old woman replied. 'Groom. My sister and I were Grooms. She married a Chisel and I married a Sidebottom.'

'And you were born in Waterslain?'

'I was.'

'And Sariel . . . well, Mr Chisel . . . he was a descendant of John Chisel.'

'That's right.'

'And he carved our missing angels.'

'So they say, dear.'

'He did. There's a display of old things in the village hall,' Annie told her. 'The Reverend Potter has put in an angel's wing and the note beside says it was carved by John Chisel. It's so lovely! I wish you could see it.'

The old woman sighed. 'And I wish I could help you both,' she said.

'Is there anything,' Annie pressed her, 'anything at all you know about the angels? Anything that could help us?'

Josie Sidebottom disappeared even deeper into her armchair. 'I can't say there is,' she replied. 'At least . . . well, Sariel did used to say his granddad's dad told him the angels were drowned.'

'Drowned!' exclaimed Annie and Sandy together.

'Drowned,' repeated the old woman.

'But why would they be?' asked Annie.

'You mean in the sea?' said Sandy. 'You mean weighed down with stones or something?'

'If someone wanted to destroy them, surely they'd just break them up,' said Annie.

'And use them as firewood,' Sandy added. 'Or is it to do with the church roof? I mean, it's like the hull of a boat. Upside down.'

Josie Sidebottom closed her eyes. 'You two know much more than I do,' she said.

'I'm sorry, Mrs Sidebottom,' Annie apologised. 'We're tiring you out.'

'In the old days,' Josie Sidebottom told them,

75

'nothing at all went to waste. Clothes got handed down from sibling to sibling. An old biscuit tin: first you ate the biscuits, then you used the tin. For marbles, or jigsaw pieces. Anything.'

Mrs Sidebottom pointed up at her rafters, and a strange, chunky, curved piece of wood between them. 'See that? It's part of the underside of an old wagon.'

'So what you're saying, ma'am,' Sandy said, 'is we may find parts of the angels used in other ways.'

'Yes, dear.'

'I get it.'

'No,' said Annie, shaking her head. 'No. What I think is they escaped, and they're still the same, still beautiful. That, or the bullies and bruisers and crooks chopped them into little pieces.'

Mrs Sidebottom looked at Annie and Sandy. 'I wish I could help you both,' she said again. 'I did have another visitor from Waterslain.'

Annie frowned.

'Long hair.'

'What colour?'

'Dark, very greasy. Alan . . .' The old woman faltered. 'Lion . . . cheetah . . .'

'Alan Leppard!' cried Annie.

'You know him, dear?'

'Sort of,' said Annie, and she shivered.

'He said he was on the look-out for the angels and he thought Sariel might be able to help him.'

'Did you tell him?' asked Annie. 'About them being drowned?'

Mrs Sidebottom shook her head. 'I didn't quite trust him, dear. Yes, and he asked me to give him a tinkle if anyone else came over about the angels.'

'Ring him?' exclaimed Annie. 'No! I mean, please don't.'

'You don't want me to, dear?'

'There's no need,' said Sandy. 'We can tell him ourselves.'

Josie Sidebottom gave Annie and Sandy a keen look. She could see the mention of the garage man had made them very nervous. Then the old woman began to work her way forward until she was sitting on the edge of her armchair. She put one hand on each faded arm and slowly levered herself up.

At that moment, the front doorbell rang.

'Osmosis!' said Sandy.

'Os-what?' asked Annie.

'Osmosis! My mom always knows when to butt out and when to show up.'

Josie Sidebottom wagged a finger at Annie and Sandy. 'Be careful!' she warned them.

'Why?' they asked. 'What of?'

The front doorbell rang again.

'I don't know exactly,' said Josie Sidebottom, 'but I can feel it in my bones. You're fishing in deep waters.'

12

Even before she stepped into the church, Annie could hear the clock ticking. She knew there wasn't much time left. She knew there was almost no time at all.

When she opened the little oak door, the latch clicked and sang out. She was sure Smasher's men would hear her, but they were making too much noise of their own. At once Annie dropped on to her hands and knees behind the back pew. Then she crawled over to the vestry and watched them through a moth-hole in the baize curtains.

One man was swinging a sledgehammer with an iron head. Whack! WHACK! She couldn't see what he was attacking.

'Gotcha!' he yelled.

Annie flinched.

Another man with a cut-throat razor was advancing on the painting of the Virgin Mary, the one where Gabriel the angel is telling her, 'Fear not, Mary: for thou has found favour with God.'

Annie knew those words off by heart. But the painting found no favour at all with the man with the cut-throat. He actually spat at it, and then he slashed it. After that, the man pulled a large nail out of one of his pockets, and with it he gouged out Mary's lovely forget-me-not blue eyes.

No! cried Annie inside her head, desolate and tearless. No! No! But there was nothing at all she could do about it.

Behind Annie, there was a high, insistent whistling, and she knew immediately what it was. She turned round and there, tucked into one corner of the vestry, was an angel. She recognised it—the faded eyes, the pale unlined skin. It was Miss McQueen.

'Sshh!' breathed the angel, like the rushes on the marsh when, soft and sharp, they're whispering to the wind. 'Sh!'

Annie rounded her dark eyes, and nodded, and quickly looked away.

One of Smasher's men was carrying a pot of paint, and carelessly slopping it. The church's tiled floor was covered with spots black as marsh mud. Then he dipped in his brush, and began to paint characters and whole words over Annie's favourite painting of all, the one in which Jesus looks so forgiving and yet so sad. Christ the Man of Sorrows.

No! cried Annie. Please! No!

Annie pressed one eye to the moth-hole, but she couldn't make out what any of the words were. But when she looked at the painter again, she recognised at once who it was. Pitterpatter. He had done his damnedest with the painting of Jesus and now he was splashing paint all over himself. He was black from head to foot.

'I'm a sort-of marsh angel,' he trumpeted. 'A dark angel.'

Annie heard the angel-whistling for a second time. She crept out between the curtains, and crouched behind the font. As soon as all the men's backs were turned, she cautiously stood up, and at once she saw a chubby little angel hiding inside the font. The little boy that Alan Leppard was selling in Baker's.

'Sshh!' breathed the little angel in a sort-of drowned voice—the sound the Carters' kettle

79

made when it was on the hob and just beginning to sing.

Annie widened her sloe-black eyes and quickly looked away. That was when she saw the west wall of the church was completely covered with large postage-stamps. Each portrayed an angel—angels announcing, angels warning, angels crossing their hands, angels playing little harps, angels spreading their azure and gold and burned orange and ash-grey wings.

When Annie looked more closely, one of the angels (the one next to the steps leading up to the tower) very slowly and carefully winked at her.

'Oh!' gasped Annie. She stared at the angel, dark-eyed, gave a quick nod and lowered her eyes.

Annie turned round to see where Smasher's men were, but they had all gone. There was no sign of them, nothing but the silence where their foul noise had been, that and the stink of their sweat, and the terrible mangle they left behind them—the precious life-work of wood-carvers and sculptors and painters and blacksmiths.

As Annie sadly gazed into the gloom of the church, the upside-down hull of the hammerbeam roof lifted a little. Then it started to turn itself over. Slowly it revolved. It righted itself.

Annie leaned the church ladder against the hull of the boat and climbed up. And as soon as she stepped aboard, she saw that all the angels were at their stations, like heavenly oarsmen, waiting for her.

Beneath her feet, she could feel the tug of the tide. She could hear the old timbers creaking and groaning. The bleached old boat swayed, then it lifted, and Annie began to wake.

13

'It's time for a full search. Inch by inch.'

That's what Sandy had told Annie in a low voice in the back of the car as Gracie drove them home to Waterslain.

'When I asked Miss McQueen about the angels while you were away,' confided Annie, 'she said I had to find out everything I possibly can, and then imagine. She said my imagining would guide me.'

And as soon as they met in the church next morning, Annie began, 'The answer's here, in this church, somewhere. That's what I think. And I think the angels want us to find them.'

Sandy stuck out his lower lip. 'Rearranged,' he said.

'You mean like the underside of that old wagon?' Annie asked. 'The one up in the rafters.'

'Yes, like that,' said Sandy. 'Changed somehow. Or invisible. I don't know.'

'I dreamed about them last night,' said Annie, 'all hiding in different places.'

'What did Mrs S. mean?' Sandy asked her. 'Drowned . . . fishing in deep waters . . . Does she know more than she's letting on?'

Annie narrowed her eyes. 'Leppard. I didn't like the sound of that.'

'Nope.'

'Pitterpatter was in my dream too, splashing black paint everywhere. He was a dark angel.'

'A dark angel,' mused Sandy. 'And a Black Book. Those words in the margin. And Josie Sidebottom . . .'

'And Leppard selling the little angel at Baker's
. . . Yes, and the wing itself, and everything Miss
McQueen told me—about Cromwell and Smasher
Dowsing.'

'Lots of clues,' said Sandy. 'We've just got to put
them together. Let's have a real careful look
round.'

'Have you seen the man in armour?' Annie
asked him, walking up to the stone effigy behind
the organ. 'With his bashed-up nose?'

'Poor guy,' said Sandy. 'Looks like a footballer.'

'A rugby player, you mean. My dad says they
break all their bones.'

Sandy frowned. 'No! A tackler! A linebacker.'

'Anyhow,' said Annie, 'he was coshed with a
sledgehammer, I know he was.'

'Up on that wall,' said Sandy, 'there are bits of
colour.'

Annie looked. 'That's just damp,' she said.
'Those sort-of salty, yellow-grey patches. The same
as behind the organ.'

'I don't mean them,' Sandy replied. 'Higher up.
Small as nickels.'

'Whattles?'

'Coins, dumb-bell!'

Annie craned her neck. 'You're right,' she
agreed. 'There must have been a painting up there
once. Before it was whitewashed.'

'And bits have shone through,' said Sandy. 'Like
searchlights.'

'You're weird! Bits of whitewash flaked off,
most likely.'

'Come on,' said Sandy. 'We've got to case each
wall inch by inch.'

'And over our heads,' said Annie, 'and beneath

82

our feet.'

The more carefully Annie and Sandy looked the more they began to notice. Three uneven tiles that rocked when you stood on the scruffy old rug covering them; and a slab of limestone, long as a coffin, missing its brass—the memorial of a lord or a lady or a rector.

'Smasher's men ripped brasses up,' Annie told Sandy. 'Look! You can still see some of the old pins.'

Annie and Sandy found more vermilion spots low down on the north wall—they looked like stars of congealed blood. They found a recess in the wall that looked like a bread oven; they found a tombstone slab without any words on it, and a board with the ten commandments on it and paintings of little angels in each corner. But they found nothing that really looked like a clue, let alone anywhere the missing angels could be hiding. They weren't in the vestry or in the font. And there were no postage-stamps on the west wall, not even one. All last night's angels had disappeared again.

Then Annie and Sandy came to the tablets.

'Wow!' exclaimed Sandy.

'Crikey!' exclaimed Annie. 'The wreckers made a real mess of these.'

Affixed to the south wall at head-height were three stone tablets, and they were all split and chipped so you could only read a few of the words and numbers.

'This one,' said Annie, 'is in memory of S-A-M . . . Samuel . . . P-O-S-T . . . Poston.'

'Paston,' Sandy corrected her.

'Paston, yes. That's a Norfolk name.'

'And here's Will . . .' Sandy pointed to the middle tablet. 'William. Must be.'

'Not necessarily,' Annie disagreed. 'It could be Willa.'

'That's not a name.'

'It is!' said Annie indignantly. 'My sister's Willa.'

'Weird,' said Sandy.

'Or Willis,' added Annie. 'There's a boy at school called Willis.'

'OK,' conceded Sandy. 'Will . . . erected by his wife Tabitha. Here's a date, look. 1642.'

'Really?' exclaimed Annie. 'That's the year before Smasher started work. Miss McQueen told me.'

'Anyhow,' said Sandy. 'These aren't clues.'

'There must be one in the church somewhere,' Annie mused.

'Yeah. Some kind of clue—or even an elegy.'

'A what?'

'For when someone's dead. Or missing. A sort of song.'

'Like your dad, you mean?' asked Annie.

Sandy didn't reply.

'No one's died on me like that,' Annie said. 'Well, my guinea pig did. That was really sad.'

'Yeah,' said Sandy.

'That's not the same, though.'

'What's so weird is he survived all the dangerous bombing missions and then crashed after the war was over.'

'How old were you?' asked Annie.

'Three.'

'Only three?'

Sandy nodded.

'Can you remember him?'

'Sometimes I think I can. Not really. But sometimes I think that if I listened the right way, I could hear him.'

'So him and your mum were only married . . .'

'Two years,' said Sandy, and he sniffed. 'Two, nearly. OK, what about this pulpit, then?'

'You ought to know,' said Annie.

'Why?'

'You hid in it.'

'Looks like a cup on a stalk.'

'It's a wine-glass pulpit,' Annie explained. 'That's what it's called. It's even older than our angels.'

'Yeah?'

'You see this side? I know the painting's scraped and scratched . . .'

'Just about everything is,' Sandy replied. 'Just about everything's been done over.' He peered at the painted panel. 'Sandpapered, sort of.'

'I know,' said Annie, 'but you can still see most of it. My dad told me this man here is John Goldale. He went out into the marsh in the dark, and stole hundreds of oysters.'

'Ugh! I hate shellfish.'

'In 1446.'

'Heck!' exclaimed Sandy. 'That's . . . nine years before John Chisel carved the angels. Chisel and Goldale: the two guys must have known each other.'

'I wouldn't go out through the marsh in the dark,' Annie went on, 'not unless it was an emergency. It's easy to lose your way, and end up in the mud.'

'You're telling me,' said Sandy.

'And there's the ghost.'

'What ghost?'

'At the ford. Where the stream runs into the marsh. The ghost of the farmer killed by two highwaymen.'

'Says who?'

Annie narrowed her eyes at Sandy. 'And there are night-boggarts and bogles,' she said in a quiet, dark voice.

'Oh yeah?'

'There are. And will-o'-the-wykes.'

Through his goggles, Sandy's gauzy grey eyes looked twice their usual size. 'And Wee Willie Winkies,' he said, smiling.

'They're shining spirits, flitting around,' Annie told him. 'And Dead . . . Dead Hands. There are. I've seen them.'

Annie grabbed her right wrist, and held up her hand. Then she flopped it and slowly waved it like a dead fish in front of Sandy's face, and that shut him up for a bit.

'Have you heard about Long Tom?' she asked him

'Who?'

'Long Tom Pattison.' Annie lowered her eyes, remembering. 'The boys saw Long Tom, they did, standing by the willow-snag, with his face white as death and staring eyes. He was holding on to the snag with one hand. The other was stretched out, gripped by a Hand without a body. Rotting flesh was dripping off its bones. The Hand pulled Tom, it pulled him with terrible strength towards the black bog next to the path. More and more strongly the Hand pulled . . .'

'That's just a story,' Sandy said. 'What happened?'

86

'Wouldn't you like to know,' Annie replied. 'It got ripped off. Long Tom's hand did.'

'You're kidding!'

'It did. And after that, Tom sat in the sun all day long, or sat by the fire, grinning and grinning. And all night long he wandered beside the edge of the marsh, screeching and moaning.'

'Whew!'

At this moment, a sack of wind walloped the north wall of the church, and all the little leaded panes groaned. No more than half a minute later, the rain began to spit, then to slap and sheet against the flint.

'It's as noisy as down by the sluice gate,' Annie called out. 'And so dark. Like the lights have gone out.'

'The lamps were going out all over Europe,' Sandy announced in a sepulchral voice.

'What?'

'The lamps! It's what someone read at my dad's memorial service. My mom gave me the service-sheet. "The lamps were going out all over Europe, and Bruce Boroff helped to light them again"'

'That's lovely,' said Annie.

'It is,' said Sandy gravely. 'I keep the sheet in a little box with my dad's wings.'

'Wings!' exclaimed Annie.

'His service badge,' said Sandy, blinking. 'And his creed: "I am an American airman: wingman, leader, warrior." And I've got a photo of him in uniform.'

Annie and Sandy stumbled around in the gloom. Then Annie tried to turn on the light by the door, but it didn't work.

'I know,' said Sandy. 'Let's climb the tower.'

'You can't.'

'It'll be lighter up there.'

'You can't, Sandy.'

'Why not?'

'Look!' Annie pointed at the notice.

DANGER

KEEP

OUT

'Can't you read?'

'Words!' replied Sandy scornfully. 'Words words words. Why are you always so obedient?'

'I'm not,' said Annie. 'The first four steps are missing.'

'It's probably all right after that,' Sandy replied.

Then Annie remembered promising her mother not to go anywhere near the church at all. 'My mum says there's a swarm of wild bees up in the tower,' she said.

'What if the angels are up there too?' Sandy asked. 'On their way up to angel height. Are you afraid?'

'Me?' exclaimed Annie.

'We gotta find out,' said Sandy. He put a hand on the tall ladder leaning against the wall. 'Are we going to need this?'

Annie twisted her right forefinger into her temple. 'Are you going to bend it or something?

The steps go round and round.'

Sandy grinned. 'Duh!' he said.

'Actually,' said Annie, 'we could prop the ladder up over the missing steps.'

Annie went up first, but when she stepped off the ladder, she could feel the fifth and sixth steps were very shallow and crumbly. Then her left foot slipped and she sprayed grit and dust into Sandy's face. Sandy made a strangled, choking noise.

After that, the steep little steps twisted up and away into the dark and Annie had to rely on her fingers and elbows and knees. Up she went, up, sidestepping on each shallow step.

'It smells disgusting,' she called out, and she was shocked by how loud her voice sounded. Loud and yet dead.

'Pigeon shit,' said the voice below her. 'It's all over my hands. Heck! What was that?'

'What?'

'That noise! Down in the church.'

'I didn't hear it,' Annie replied. 'All I can hear is rain—rain, and our dead voices.'

'A sort of bang.'

'What?'

'It must have been the door. Someone coming in.'

'They won't hear us, not with all this rain,' Annie said.

'Sshh!' Sandy cautioned her.

'It's so tight up here,' Annie said more quietly. 'Like these steps are made for pygmies or something. There's only just enough room.'

'Tea for two,' warbled the voice below her, sounding quite unearthly. 'Nobody near us to see us or hear us. No friends or relations. Nobody to

89

scare us. Whoo-hoo! Whoo-hoo!'

'Hey!' exclaimed Annie. 'It's getting lighter.' She scrabbled and scrambled up a few more steps, and sprayed Sandy with grit and muck again.

'Uch! Slowly, can't you? I'm waiting here until you're right up.'

'There's a room up here, with all the slitty windows.'

Annie felt as if she'd been blind all her life and was somehow able to see again. She wiped her watering eyes on the back of her filthy sleeve. Quickly she climbed and laid both hands on the wooden platform at the top of the steps. There were two curved white things, murmuring and hanging like folded wings from the rafter in front of her. White and shining, almost glowing, and peppered with black spots. Annie tiptoed towards them, enchanted, trying to see what they were; but then she tripped over her own feet. She yelled, and reached out, and fell flat on her face.

At once, above the sound of the rain, Annie heard a whirring, a hoarse droning—and then an angry buzzing.

The moment she picked herself up from the shaky wooden platform, a bee flew straight at her face. It haloed her head, touched down, and stung her on the neck. That most tender part, just behind her right ear.

'Ow!' complained Annie.

At first, the sting felt no worse than a pinprick. But then it began to burn, and Annie became frightened.

'I'm coming down!' she called in a pained voice. 'I've been stung.'

'You can't,' said Sandy. 'I'm coming up.' And

with that, he grabbed the edge of the platform, and hauled himself into the little room at the top of the tower.

'I've been stung,' Annie told him again. 'Look, the whole place is swirling with them.'

A second guard-bee smelt the first sting, arrowed towards it, and stung Annie on her collar-bone. Then a third smelt the first and second stings, and stung Annie on her right wrist as she clamped her hand over her neck. Annie screwed up her eyes. She could feel the bees' tiny wings tickling her skin before they stung her.

'Down!' she sobbed. 'Down, Sandy!'

Sandy didn't know whether to go down into the dark backwards or try to turn round and go forwards. Down he bumped, first grazing his elbows, then turning and twisting his left knee, and on her bottom Annie slid after him.

The stream of bees streamed down the stone steps and attacked every part of Annie they could get at. They tangled in her hair. They stung her bare legs. Her ankles. Her arms. Her face.

Annie wailed. She screamed.

Dozens of bees, meanwhile, flew over Annie's head and dived on to Sandy. One stung him on the back of his neck. One got inside his Aertex shirt. One crawled inside his spectacles and stung him on his right eyelid.

Sandy yelled. He howled.

Down the stone steps Annie and Sandy clattered and slipped and stumbled, pursued by the whizzing wild bees. They stung Annie on her tongue and her left eyelid and in the crook of her right arm; they stung Sandy on both heels and in his groin. The furious bees drove them down and

91

out of their high stronghold.

Two men were standing in the nave. One was wearing a dog-collar, the other an oily boiler-suit, and both heard the hullabaloo in the tower.

For a moment, each of them supposed some bird or animal was trapped, or the barn owl had brought back a rabbit, still alive and shrieking. But then they heard all the clattering and howling.

'What in the name of God . . .' exclaimed the Reverend Potter. His bushy right eyebrow leaped up and down and he hurried to the foot of the stone steps leading up to the tower. No sooner had he bent sideways and peered up into the gloom than the two children tumbled out of the tower. Sandy first, then Annie on top of him.

Several dozen angry bees pursued them. They stormed out into the body of the church, whirring and buzzing.

Annie and Sandy lay on the stone floor, terrified, clutching themselves and whimpering.

'Quick, Alan!' urged the rector. 'The vestry curtains.'

Alan Leppard strode across to the vestry and ripped down the green baize. Then the two men flapped away the bees and rolled Annie in one curtain, Sandy in the other.

'Drat!' said the rector, clapping a hand to his pink ear lobe.

'Little sods!' said Leppard.

The bees heard him and at once one stung him on his lower lip.

'Heck!' yelled the garage man. He swiped the bee with the flat of his hand and missed. 'Little sod!'

'Come on,' said the rector. 'Out of here.'

The Reverend Potter picked up Sandy, Alan Leppard picked up Annie. In his strong greasy arms, he cradled her.

Without a word they carried the two moaning children out of the church and through the rain. They hurried down to the lych-gate and Alan's waiting car.

'Doctor Grant's,' said the rector. 'As quick as you can. This could be serious, Alan.'

14

That night, the wind dropped but still the rain danced. Not spiteful, not sharp as pins and needles, and not slapping the flint walls of the Carters' little cottage. Just a cool, soft wash. At times little more than a gauzy mist enveloping Waterslain and the breathing marsh.

An angel came and stood by Annie's bed.

Annie tried to roll over on to her back so she could see it better, but then she realised she couldn't move at all. She couldn't even move her head. She felt as if she were bound from top to toe like a mummy. All she could do was open her eyes very wide and look up at the angel out of the corners of them. Your fingers are so long, she thought.

Annie couldn't quite tell whether the angel was a girl or a boy.

I saw you in the tower, Annie thought. I did, didn't I? Your white wings. White and shining. Are you made of light?

The angel smiled a tender smile.

A girl-boy, that's what you are. But your wings aren't ochre or silver or gold or vermilion. They're almost glowing.

'Don't you want us to find you?' Annie said out loud. At least, that's what she tried to say, but her tongue was so swollen she could only make blobby sounds: 'Glute choutuz ter foid je.'

Poor Annie was tongue-tied and she wanted to talk to the angel so much. I tripped over my own feet, I tripped and I stumbled. You know we're searching for you. We are, everywhere. Are you all hiding up there in the tower? I stumbled, I fell—I haven't got wings like you.

In her half-sleep, Annie tossed and whimpered. Everything hurts so much. I'm burning all over.

The angel was holding something between its hands. It broke off a piece and reached out, and laid it on Annie's tongue.

What is it, wondered Annie. Sweet. So sweet. I know! It's honeycomb.

The honey soothed Annie's swollen tongue, and trickled down her throat and made her cough a bit.

Around the cottage the August rain murmured. Somewhere out on the marsh one night-bird cried out, another answered. In the ghost-light of Annie's bedroom, the angel spread its shining wings and laid its cool right hand on Annie's blazing forehead.

Its voice was so clear. Innocent as water just raised from a well.

'We are waiting for you.'

15

For three days it rained.

'Blast!' said Mr Carter. 'Something's up with the fronts and behinds.'

'What's that, Tom?'

'The weather fronts, Margie. Flaming July? That rained all month. And August's not much better.'

'But not a drop in April,' added Mrs Carter. 'It's arsy-versy.'

'It is and all,' Mr Carter agreed. 'Pools and sheets all over the place. Next thing, the Ghost Beck will flood.'

'That went right through the cellars last time. All of a sudden.'

Tom Carter grinned. 'And washed the labels off all the pub's wine bottles.'

'Dangerous, though,' added Margie Carter.

For three days it rained in the parish of Waterslain, and for three days Annie and Sandy tossed on their beds of pain. When the Reverend Potter called in to see how Annie was doing, Mrs Carter told him all about Annie's and Sandy's quest for the angels, and how it was getting completely out of hand, and how she and Mr Carter didn't want Annie going up anywhere near the church again. Doctor Grant, meanwhile, dropped in to see Annie and Sandy twice each day, as soon as his morning surgery was over, and again in the early evening. And each time he came, he checked their poor swollen faces and arms and legs.

'Fourteen stings each,' he pronounced. And to Gracie, he added, 'Sandy's had a narrow escape, what with his asthma. If his throat and mouth had swollen like Annie's, he wouldn't have been able to breathe.'

'I burn all over,' Annie told the doctor. 'And itch.'

'That's what happens,' he replied. 'The venom spreads. It travels up your veins.'

'Everywhere,' said Annie in a listless, dreamy voice. 'Why did they sting us like that?'

'The bees were guarding their homes,' the doctor explained, 'where they store their honey, and their queen lays her eggs. You must have disturbed them.'

'I didn't mean to,' said Annie, and she closed her aching eyes.

'Now be sure to dab on more calamine four times a day,' Doctor Grant told Margie Carter and Gracie. 'It'll stop the itching and bring down their fever.'

For most of the time, Annie drowsed. But sometimes she reached up with both hands and clutched her wrists and gabbled words and half-words. Once, Mrs Carter heard Annie call out, clear as a bell, 'Wait! Wait!'

'Yes, love, yes,' Mrs Carter whispered. Treading as lightly as she could on the creaky floorboards, she laid a cool sponge on Annie's forehead. 'We're waiting. Come back soon.'

For three days it rained, and Anni_____d and Mrs Carter bided her time an_____ tongue.

This, however, was more than s_____ the waiting room of Doctor _____ immediately after Annie and Sandy had been stung.

'I knew there'd be trouble with you, Gracie Dune. I knew it.'

'Lay off me.'

'You piece of fluff! Making eyes at Tom.'

Gracie spread her painted nails like claws. 'I'm not having that, you old cow. You lay off me, Margie Carter.'

The door between the waiting room and the surgery opened, and Doctor Grant put his head round it.

'You're out of breath,' he observed. 'Both of you.'

'My nerves, doctor,' Mrs Carter replied. 'How's Annie? Is she all right?'

'Annie and Sandy are asleep. That's natural, because of the shock.' The doctor gave the two mothers a kind look without actually smiling. 'No, Annie's not all right,' he said, 'and neither's Sandy. They've both been stung all over.'

Mrs Carter clapped her hand over her mouth.

'It's wait-and-see,' Doctor Grant told them. 'If their fever starts to come down tomorrow, all well and good.'

'What if it doesn't?' asked Mrs Carter.

'I'll transfer them.'

'Transfer them?' asked Gracie.

'To the Cottage Hospital.'

'I was just saying to Mrs Boroff,' Margie Carter began, still rather breathless, 'we can't have them going up to the church again.'

Gracie nodded vigorously, and then patted her silken blonde hair. 'That's right,' she said.

'Annie did promise,' Mrs Carter began, 'but I

expect . . . well, Sandy . . .'

'Sandy didn't know nothing about the bees,' objected Gracie. 'I didn't neither.'

'No,' said Margie Carter. 'Well, you wouldn't, would you.'

'It's that wing,' said Gracie.

'It is,' said Mrs Carter. 'Those blessed angels! And you encouraging them, driving over to Diss, and all. Well, Tom and I are putting a stop to it, and that's that.'

'Now come in to the surgery,' Doctor Grant said in a calm voice. 'And don't be surprised. I've turned them both pasty white.'

'White?' repeated Mrs Carter and Gracie.

'Bicarbonate of soda,' Doctor Grant said. 'The only good treatment for bee stings. Bicarb first to relieve the stings, and then calamine lotion.'

On the morning of the fourth day, the watery sun kept glaring between the skidding, jaundiced clouds and Annie felt a good deal better. She got up for breakfast and, after her mother had popped a thermometer under her tongue, she sipped a mug of Bovril and dipped two soldiers of toast into it. Mrs Carter watched her and licked her lips.

'You remember what I said?' she asked. 'Young lady?'

Annie sniffed. She knew what was coming.

' "The bees buzz and fizz like nobody's business, and if you bother them, they'll sting you to death in two minutes." Remember?'

Annie sniffed again.

'Little howitzers!' Mrs Carter paused to let her words sink in. 'You promised me, Annie! You promised you wouldn't go anywhere near the churchyard.'

Annie stared into her Bovril.

'Didn't you?'

'Yes.'

'You're getting too big for your boots, young lady.'

Annie shook her head miserably.

'You are! If Alan and the Reverend hadn't rescued you . . .'

Annie frowned and looked up.

'Alan Leppard. He rolled you in baize, and carried you out of the church, and drove you down to Doctor Grant.'

'Alan did?' Annie stared dolefully into her Bovril again. 'What was he doing in the church?'

'How should I know? I told you the Reverend's giving him odd jobs, you know, cleaning out the Rectory attic, and things like that. He's probably asked Alan to service the heating system.'

Annie could feel her eyes growing hot with tears. How could she ever find the angels when Alan was snooping around after them the whole time?

'In fact,' said Annie's mother, 'I did hear the Reverend has asked Alan to join the PCC.'

'What's that?'

'The Parochial Church Council,' Mrs Carter replied. 'Your dad and I have been talking. You're not going anywhere near the church again.'

'I am,' said Annie in a low voice.

'I beg your pardon?'

Annie pressed her lips together and gave her mother a defiant look.

'Do you understand?' Mrs Carter insisted.

'Mum,' whispered Annie, and silently she began to weep. Her tears ran down her cheeks and dropped into her toast. Her shoulders shook.

Mrs Carter permitted herself one last salvo. 'Next thing,' she said, 'you'll go down into that old tunnel, and get lost or something.'

Annie pricked up her ears. What tunnel, she thought.

Mrs Carter shook her head in vexation and bit her lower lip. 'Now promise me, Annie. Promise you won't go near the church again.'

Annie gave a loud sniff and nodded her head.

'And if you want to see that shrimp again, if that's the real reason, bring him round ours, or go out on the marsh. You understand?'

Annie nodded again.

'Anyhow,' Mrs Carter finished off, 'Willa and Storm get in late this afternoon, and you'll have your hands full. Back to bed with you now! Stay in bed until lunchtime.'

As she traipsed upstairs and back to bed, Annie knew she was going to disobey her mother. And immediately after lunch, saying she was going to see Miss McQueen to ask her something about William Dowsing . . .

'Who?' asked her mother.

'Everyone called him Smasher,' Annie replied.

'Never heard of him.'

. . . after fibbing to her mother, Annie headed straight for the church. She just doesn't understand, she thought. I know my mum's worried about me, but this is really important.

Inside the church again, Annie began to feel much more hopeful. Several times she heard the angel's water-voice chiming, 'We are waiting for you.' And she felt sure Smasher's men hadn't destroyed the angels and they really were hiding

101

somewhere very near. She was certain that she and Sandy must have missed some vital clue.

Is it in the Black Book in the vestry chest, she wondered? *'Pd to John Chisel for carving 14 angels and erecting in roof . . .'* What about those fly-words in the margin: 'Angels waterslain'? Or is the clue fourteen and twice fourteen? And what about Sariel's great-granddad saying the angels were drowned? Not to mention angel-flowers and angel-height, and angels being made of light? What's the truth of it?

And what about the tunnel, thought Annie. My mother didn't mean to mention it and I could tell she was cross with herself when she did. It just sort-of slipped out. A tunnel! Where does it lead to? How do you get into it?

'Oh!' cried Annie. 'I know! Of course I know!'

At this moment, the church door latch lifted. Annie jumped, and Sandy stepped in. His face was pale white, still pasted with calamine lotion.

'Sandy!' cried Annie, and her cheeks turned pink. She couldn't believe how pleased she was to see him.

'I'm invisible again,' Sandy told her.

'What do you mean?'

'I'm not here. At least, I'm not allowed to be.'

'Neither am I,' Annie replied. 'My mum and dad don't understand.'

'Parents can be a real drag,' Sandy said. 'Still, at least you've got two of them.'

'Oh, Sandy!'

'When you've only got one . . . well, my mum went ape, banging on at me the whole time.'

'My mum was furious too,' Annie told him.

'That's because she's afraid.'

102

'Those sheets of wax . . .' began Annie.

'The honeycombs?'

'Yes, white and hanging like that. They looked like folded wings. Anyhow, are you all right?'

Sandy looked at Annie through his spectacles. 'I'm pasty white,' he said. He smiled faintly. 'Pooped! Like I've been ill for months.'

'Same here. Doctor Grant told my mum you could have got . . . ana . . . ana . . . I can't remember the name. It gives you frothy saliva and bad breath and diarrhoea and . . .'

'Anaphylaxis,' said Sandy. 'Get that and you're a stiff.'

'What?'

'A corpse.'

'Did your mum tell you about Alan?' Annie asked.

'What about him?'

'Helping to save us. Him and Pitterpatter.'

Sandy gave a low whistle. 'What was he doing here, then?'

'Exactly,' said Annie.

'What's going on?' asked Sandy, slowly shaking his head. 'I don't like it.'

'Neither do I,' said Annie. 'Snooping around, searching for our angels, keeping a watch on us. He scares me.' She shivered slightly, and then she began to scratch under her right ear.

'Don't,' said Sandy in a stern voice.

'It itches.'

'Me too.'

Annie grabbed a tuft of Sandy's hair on the side of his head, and tweaked it.

'Don't!' complained Sandy loudly.

'That's a bee sting,' said Annie. 'That's what we

all call it. Actually, we play a bee-game—me and Polly and Daisy and everyone—when there's a new girl at school. We did when Geraldine came last year.'

'Who?'

'Alan's daughter.'

Sandy didn't seem very interested. He wandered across to the south side of the church, and stood there in a shaft of sunlight.

'Don't you want to know?' asked Annie. 'We tell the new girl she's our Queen Bee and we're her worker bees. She has to ask us to go and fetch honey—well, pollen—and bring it back to her. Then we all run off to the washroom, and fill our mouths with water.'

'I geddit.'

'And then we run back to the Queen Bee and spit it out into her face.'

'Do you see what I see?' Sandy asked.

A second shaft of sunlight was arrowing down on to the wall, just under one of the shattered stone tablets, and Sandy was pointing at it.

'Letters,' said Sandy. 'Someone's scratched something on the wall.'

'They're so faint,' Annie said. 'Almost rubbed out.'

The letters and words looked like dark shivers on shining water, or the little lines left by speedy waterboatmen.

Sandy stood so close to the wall that the tip of his nose was almost touching it.

'How come we didn't see them before?' asked Annie.

Sandy made a strange humming noise, but not like a bee. 'Maybe you can only see them . . .' He held up his left hand like a policeman, and stopped the sunshaft, and at once the words on the dun wall disappeared.

'Clever,' said Annie.

'Anyhow,' Sandy added, 'they don't really look like letters at all. Not to begin with.'

'Let me see,' said Annie.

And then, character by character, Annie and Sandy puzzled out the syllables:

Between her Will
And his Wall
Waterslain
We Lie Waiting

'We lie waiting,' said Annie. 'Sandy, what does it mean?'

Sandy didn't reply.

'It doesn't make sense.'

'It might,' said Sandy, 'if we knew what it was about. It's like a riddle.'

'Between her will and his wall . . .' mouthed Annie. 'Whose will? Whose wall?'

'And who lies waiting?' added Sandy.

'I think it's about the angels.'

'Mebbe.'

'Waterslain we lie,' said Annie. 'That doesn't make sense. How can you lie Waterslain?'

'I dunno.'

Waiting, remembered Annie. Waiting. We are waiting for you.

'But I'll find out,' said Sandy.

'Oh, Sandy! I haven't even told you yet.'

'Told me what?'

'My mother let on—by mistake! There's a

105

tunnel.' Annie led the way back across the church to the scruffy rug and the loose tiles. 'And I'm dead certain I know where it is.'

Annie pulled back the rug with a flourish, and dropped it in a heap, and got down on her knees.

'Ow!' she exclaimed. 'I've got a sting on my right knee. Do you know how many stings we got?'

'No,' said Sandy.

'Fourteen. Fourteen each. Isn't that weird?'

Annie was working her fingers round one of the loose tiles and Sandy gingerly lowered himself on to his knees beside her.

'It's loose,' said Annie. 'It's coming.' She managed to grip one corner of the tile, and pulled it right up.

'OK,' said Sandy. 'That's the difficult one.'

Shoulder to shoulder, Annie and Sandy bent over the loose tiles, and pulled them up one by one. Seven of them, dusky pink, each glazed with a black cross.

Underneath the tiles was a thin layer of grit and a wooden panel with an iron ring in it. Sandy tapped it. It was hollow.

'That's it!' cried Annie. 'It must be.'

'Gotcha!' growled a deep voice.

Annie sprang up like a jack-in-the-box. Sandy took his time.

The shadow of a big man fell over both of them. 'What are you two up to?' he demanded gruffly. It was Alan Leppard.

'Nothing,' said Annie.

'Nothing,' said the garage man. 'For starters, you shouldn't be here. Over her dead body, Annie. Over her dead body. That's what your mum told me.'

Annie quailed.

Leppard hoicked up his overalls and wiped his greasy hands on his black T-shirt. His face was grimy. 'And you, you miserable little fairy. I bet your mum said the same to you.'

'She didn't, actually,' said Sandy. He peered at the garage man through his specs, and blinked. 'You look like an angel of death or something.'

Annie held her breath, but the garage man ignored Sandy's brave words.

'Want me to tell your parents then, do you?'

'No,' Annie said loudly.

'What's it got to do with you?' Sandy demanded.

'First the tower . . .' began Leppard. 'Planning a trip into the tunnel now, are we?'

'No!' said Annie.

The garage man spat on the floor and rubbed the spit under his left foot. 'Two little fools, rushing in where angels fear to tread.'

'It's a quest,' Sandy explained. 'We're following clues.'

'A quest, my aunt!' Alan Leppard retorted. 'I know what you're up to.' He narrowed his dark eyes and slowly rocked forward on the balls of his feet until he was leaning right over Annie and Sandy. 'Listen to me,' he said in a low, tight voice. 'If you go down that tunnel, you won't be coming up again.'

Annie and Sandy lowered their eyes. They stared at the loose tiles, the scruffy rug.

'Got it?' demanded Leppard. 'Now buzz off, both of you! Scram!'

Outside the church door, Sandy kicked at the gravel. 'I'm not going to be scared off by that greaseball,' he said in a loud voice.

'Sshh!'

'He's got no right to stop us.'

'So why does he want to?' asked Annie.

'Exactly,' Sandy agreed. 'Did you hear what he said? He threatened us.'

'They're down there,' said Annie.

'Mebbe.'

'We've got to save them.'

'And I gotta go,' Sandy told her. 'Fast! Mom and I are driving into Hunst'n.'

'Oh no!' moaned Annie. 'When can we meet?'

'Tomorrow. It'll have to be.'

Annie clicked her tongue. 'Willa and Storm are coming.'

'Who?'

'And they're staying for a whole week. I told you, Willa's my half-sister, and she's married to Rod and he's a sailor. Storm's my nephew and he's only three.'

'Oh, yeah.'

'And when they come, I'm his babysitter.'

'Bring him up here then!' Sandy told her. 'Sit him up here. After breakfast.' He gave Annie a watery smile and took off with a strange, loping stride, waving both hands as he went, rather like a giant squid.

16

A few minutes later, Annie ran into Miss McQueen walking along the green lane between the village street and the church.

'I was on my way to see you,' Annie said brightly.

The corners of Miss McQueen's lips twitched. 'A strange way to come, dear.'

'No, I was. I told my mum I was. I can come another day.'

Miss McQueen nodded. 'That would be better,' she said. 'When I'm not on my constitutional.'

'Consti-what?' asked Annie.

'My little walk. A walk to benefit the health. Yes, and how about your health, Annie? All your stings.'

'Oh! Who told you?'

'Half of Waterslain! Jem did, when I was buying myself a nice pork chop. Sue, at the Post Office . . . Teresa . . . Are you all right now?'

'Sandy and I—you know, he's the American boy—we got fourteen stings each and they itch the whole time.'

'Lavender oil,' said Miss McQueen. 'Has your mother got any?'

'I don't know.'

'I'll bring some when I come round later.'

'Oh!' exclaimed Annie.

'You'd forgotten,' said Miss McQueen looking at Annie over her half-glasses. 'Well, I'm not surprised. And you won't have been able to practise, I know. We'll just have to pick up where we left off.' She pursed her purplish mouth and sang in a reedy voice: ' "Where the bee sucks, there suck I. In a cowslip's bell I lie." Do you remember that, Annie?'

Annie nodded. 'Sucking bees are all right,' she said. 'I don't mind that kind. I'll practise it a bit before you come.'

'You must have upset them,' Miss McQueen said.

'I know. Sandy and I went up the tower, and I tripped over the wooden platform at the top.'

'Bees don't like any kind of vibration,' Miss McQueen explained. 'It upsets them. You poor girl.'

'I'm all right now,' Annie reassured her. 'We both are.'

'Well, I must get on,' said Miss McQueen. 'This green lane's like a dyke, almost.'

'What do you mean?'

'Look! With the fields half-flooded on either side. I've never seen anything like it. It's mid-August, Annie, and we're well-nigh waterslain.'

Annie frowned.

'Waterslain's half-waterslain,' Miss McQueen added with a smile.

'I'm sorry,' said Annie. 'I don't know what you mean.'

'You do know what waterslain means.'

'No.'

Miss McQueen blinked. 'Then I've failed you miserably. Waterslain, Annie, it's an old Norfolk word. It means flooded. It means drowned.'

Annie's heart began to hammer. She knew at once that she had stumbled on a vital piece of information. As soon as Miss McQueen had gone

110

on her way, she began to work things out.

For a start, thought Annie, the Black Book. Those fly-words in the margin, the ones in different writing. 'Angels waterslain.' 'Angels waterslain' not 'Waterslain angels'. Isn't that telling me our angels were drowned?

Yes, it is! Of course it is! Annie felt quite breathless. She gripped the railings on the side of the lane and stared into the floodwater.

It must be. That's what Mrs Sidebottom told us as well. Annie could see Josie Sidebottom deep inside her armchair, and hear her saying, 'Well, Sariel did used to say his granddad's dad told him the angels were drowned.'

The Black Book . . . Josie Sidebottom . . . drowned . . .

Annie hoisted herself on to the top railing and there she sat for a while between the green lane and the silver flood, this land-girl, this water-girl, in search of angels.

Those words on the church wall, she thought. The ones below the smashed tablets: Waterslain we lie waiting. Waterslain we lie waiting. That's a message, it has to be. Not from the angels—they can't write. From whoever hid them.

Annie gripped the rail and stood up. She spread her arms like pale wings.

It all adds up, she thought. It does. The Black Book and Josie Sidebottom and the words on the wall. Like pieces of a jigsaw. You look at them and look at them, then suddenly you see how they fit together. And all this, thought Annie, is because of a clue that was right under my nose. Waterslain. Slain by water. Duh!

Still standing, arms spread, Annie remembered

the angel who had stood beside her bed, and given her a piece of honeycomb.

Its voice was so clear. Innocent as water just raised from a well.

'We are waiting for you.'

They're down in the tunnel, thought Annie. That's where they are. Maybe the tunnel sometimes gets water in it and that drowns the angels. Somehow, Sandy and me and Alan have all found out at the same time, and that's why he threatened us. We've got to get there first.

'Where have you been?'

'Talking to Miss McQueen,' said Annie. 'She's bringing lavender oil round ours.'

'Whatever for?'

'My itches.'

Mrs Carter shook her head impatiently. 'Willa rang. They're in on the four o'clock bus.'

'They always are,' said Annie.

'Except when Rod's home,' her mother said. 'He likes to catch the really early bus.'

As soon as Willa and Storm stepped down from the bus, Storm propelled himself like a missile into Annie's arms. Annie scooped him up and lifted him high above her head, squealing. His dark brown hair—the same colour as hers, really—was as tousled as an old mop and his chestnut eyes fairly sparkled with mischief.

Willa kissed her mother. 'You all right, then?'

'You?' her mother replied.

Willa planted a kiss on top of Annie's head. 'Hello, sis'!'

'Mmm!' replied Annie, her face buried in Storm's midriff.

'What about those stings, then?'

112

Annie threw back her head. 'Horrible!' she exclaimed.

Willa looked around her, and stretched her arms from her rounded shoulders right down to her pretty, painted fingernails. She sniffed the damp air. 'Home!' she said with a sigh.

'That always will be,' her mother said.

'You said it's miles from anywhere,' Annie told her sister.

'It is.'

'It's not. It's everywhere! Isn't it, Storm?'

'Everywhere,' repeated Storm in a solemn voice.

'All right, then,' said Willa. 'Nowhere and everywhere.'

'And teeming with angels,' Mrs Carter added. 'Nothing but blessed angels. I'm sick to death of them.'

'Mum!' Annie complained.

'Well, I am. Missing angels and fallen angels, like Gracie Dune.'

'What are you on about?' Willa asked.

'I'm right glad you've come, I am.'

17

The next morning it was damp yet again—that kind of day when, to begin with, there's rain in the air without it actually raining. Mrs Carter and Willa decided to go shopping in Fakenham, seeing as Mr Carter felt well enough to drive them in.

'You'll look after Storm,' Mrs Carter said.

'Yes, Mum,' replied Annie.

'You're a real sport, Annie,' Willa told her.

Storm put his arms round Annie's legs, and her mother gave Annie a meaningful look. 'Mind you do, then,' she said.

Mr Carter came inside from outside. 'Blast!' he said. 'That's going to rain after all.'

'Rain! Rain!' Mrs Carter complained.

'Go away!' Annie sang out, grabbing Storm's hands and swinging him round. 'Rain! Rain! Go away! Come again another day.'

'Again!' yelled Storm.

'Rod does that,' said Willa, smiling.

'It's raining, it's raining,' sang Annie, 'it's raining on the rocks, and all the little fisher girls are lifting up their frocks.'

Willa burst out laughing.

'That's quite enough of that, young lady,' Mrs Carter said.

'Who told you that one, then?' Willa asked.

'Don't encourage her,' cautioned her mother.

'Blast!' said Mr Carter, as much to himself as to anyone else. 'The Ghost Beck must be bubbling and boiling under our feet. If that bursts, there'll be flooding right through the village.'

As soon as Annie and Storm had waved the grey Hillman Imp goodbye, Annie hurried into the kitchen and took a box of Swan Vestas out of a drawer.

'Look, Storm!' she said. She lit one match and waved it in front of him.

'Me.'

'No. Go on, then.'

But when Storm tried to light a match, he broke his in two.

Then Annie picked up the torch, the rubber-cased one, from the table by the front door.

'Raincoats,' she said to herself. 'Sou'westers. I know! Wellingtons.'

'Marsh,' said Storm with a joyous smile.

'Church first.' Annie touched her right forefinger to her lips. 'Secret.'

'Secret,' repeated Storm. Then he too raised his stubby forefinger and squashed his mouth and the tip of his nose.

*   *   *

Sandy was already waiting in the church.

'I've brought Storm,' Annie called out.

'So I see.'

Storm looked just as doubtful about Sandy as did Sandy about Storm. He reached up to Annie. 'Carry,' he said.

'Sit him up on this ledge,' said Sandy.

'There!' said Annie, lifting Storm and planting him on the ledge. 'A special window-seat.'

'Now be an angel,' added Sandy in an expressionless voice.

But Storm at once began to wiggle and wanted

115

to be lifted down.

'At this rate . . .' said Sandy. 'C'mon!'

Annie shook her head. 'He'll get used to you,' she said. 'Listen, Sandy.'

Then Annie told him about her meeting with Miss McQueen, and how she'd worked out that the Black Book and what Josie Sidebottom had said and the words scratched on the wall were all connected.

'Jeez!' said Sandy, tapping his forehead. 'Overtime.'

'I thought you'd be pleased,' said Annie. 'They're hiding in the tunnel. I know they are. And so does Alan Leppard.'

Sandy gave Storm a cautious smile. Then he ballooned his cheeks, put his forefinger into his mouth, and . . . pop!

Storm's eyes lit up, silver-bright as the sparklers in the church's leaded diamond panes. 'Again!' he urged Sandy.

'That's better,' Sandy said. 'Now keep quiet!' He frowned and pursed his lips. 'OK, but the words on the wall there—what about the Wall and Will bit?'

'I don't know exactly,' Annie said, 'but it doesn't matter anyhow. We've got to get down the tunnel.'

Sandy shook his head. 'I'm not sure they're there,' he said. 'Not if your mom and everyone know about the tunnel. It's too obvious.'

'I just hope we're not too late,' Annie went on. 'I mean, if Alan's got there first . . .'

'The crook.'

'Are we going, then?'

'Not with Storm,' said Sandy.

'We've got to. I've brought Wellingtons and

stuff.'

Sandy surveyed the raincoats and sou'westers and Wellingtons. 'Fourteen angels,' he said, frowning. 'Twenty-eight feet. Your twenty-eight Wellingtons.'

'That's right,' said Annie. 'Is it a sign, do you think?'

'What of?' said Sandy. 'A sign they were dumped in the sea?'

'You don't believe that.'

'And twenty-eight stings,' said Sandy thoughtfully.

'Weird.'

'It sure is.'

'I didn't tell you,' said Annie. 'I had a dream and all our angels were wearing waders. Come on! Are we going down?'

'Shall we lock the door?' said Sandy.

'What if someone wants to come in?' asked Annie.

'It'll stop them, dumb-bell!'

But there was no key in the church door, so Sandy kept watch outside while Annie hoicked away the scruffy rug, and sat Storm on it, and lifted the large loose tiles. Although the wooden panel was still in place, it was no longer covered with a layer of grit.

Alan's been down already, thought Annie. He has.

Annie grasped the ring, but the panel was so heavy she was only able to lift it a couple of inches. She had to let go, and the panel fell back with a thump.

'Carry,' said Storm.

'Sandy!' called Annie. 'Come and help.'

117

Then Annie took hold of the ring again, and Sandy gripped the rim of the panel and pulled it right up, until it fell over with a clatter.

Annie and Sandy peered down into the dark. Steep stone steps. Four of them. Five. Six. Seven . . . That's all they could see.

'Big adventure,' Annie told Storm. 'Big secret. Sshh! Say nothing.'

'Nothing,' agreed Storm, and he put his forefinger to his nose and lips.

Annie quickly pulled on Storm's Wellingtons, and then her own.

'I'll go first,' she said. 'I've got the torch.'

'OK,' said Sandy. 'And I'll go behind Storm.'

Annie cautiously lowered herself on to the first step. The second and the third, the fourth. But the steps were much too steep for Storm's little legs, so Annie put her hands under his shoulders and jumped him down.

A stale, sour smell from the underground enveloped the three of them. It wasn't exactly foul, but it certainly wasn't pleasant. Old urine, thought Annie. Rotting sedges and plantains. Old people, sometimes.

'First up, now down,' boomed the voice behind her. 'Down and up, up and down, halfway round the godamn town!' And then, 'At least there aren't any bees down here.'

'Carry,' begged a small voice.

'We're nearly there, Storm,' Annie said brightly, but the stone walls took the shine off her voice. 'Nearly there.'

'Jeez!' exclaimed Sandy. 'Here we are.'

A moment later, all three of them were standing in the pallor at the bottom of the steps. The quite low tunnel—no more than five feet high—was chill and very slightly draughty. It was damp. It was very quiet.

Annie played her torch on the walls. They were made of rough slabs, and oozing. The floor was earthen.

'Look!' said Sandy. 'Another iron ring. There! In the roof.'

'What's that for, then?' Annie asked. She reached up and poked at the roof of the tunnel with her fingertips and a shower of grit fell into her hair and mouth. Annie spluttered and spat out the bits.

'Carry,' beseeched the small voice beside her.

'Yes,' said Annie. 'Carry.' She scooped Storm up. 'Big secret. Sshh!'

Standing there, Annie realised that never had she been anywhere so silent. She could hear nothing at all but the sound of their own breathing. We're at coffin-level, she thought. And it must be like this inside a coffin. Except there wouldn't even be breathing and, anyhow, you wouldn't be able to hear.

A drop of water fell from the roof and scored a direct hit on the torch. It splashed onto the rubber casing, and Sandy and Annie both jumped at the sound of it.

Almost at once, they heard a nasty scuffling. An insistent scratching.

Sandy screwed up his face. 'Is that what I think it is?'

'Could be,' said Annie. 'Or coypu, maybe. Which way? Left or right?'

'Good question,' said Sandy. 'Jeez! It's cold down here.'

'W, A, left, right . . .' began Annie, drumming her fingers on Storm's forearm, 'T, E, left, right . . . R, S, left, right, L A, left, right . . . I, N, left, right. We'll go right.'

'Away from the village then,' Sandy said. 'Away from the sea.'

'And upwind, sort-of,' Annie replied. 'I can feel the draught on my cheeks.'

'How far does this tunnel go?'

'And where does it lead?' added Annie. 'Are you all right, Storm?'

'Up,' replied Storm in a miserable little voice.

'And where are our angels?' Annie said. 'They're waiting for us.'

'Give me the flashlight,' said Sandy.

'What? Oh, the torch.'

For two minutes and maybe three, Sandy led the way along the tunnel. Then he turned round to face Annie and Storm. 'Nope,' he said. 'The angels are AWOL.'

'Where are they?' puzzled Annie. 'No side passages for them to hide in.'

'No ledges for them to sit on,' said Sandy. 'I thought you were positive.'

'We haven't even got to the end of the tunnel yet.'

'I said they weren't down here. You always think you know best.'

Annie looked crestfallen. 'They won't be hiding where everyone can see them,' she said. 'Not like when Storm plays hide-and-seek, and runs a few yards away and claps his hands over his eyes, and calls out, "Ready"'

'Listen!' said Sandy.

'What?'

'Hear that?'

There was a distant growling and grumbling, the sound thunder makes when it runs round the rim of the horizon. Annie and Sandy could feel the ground vibrating under their feet.

Then the noise quickly grew much louder, immediately ahead of them. The roaring of a steam train in a dark tunnel, a dragon showering sparks, and belching smoke, and roaring. Louder, louder now, a snarling and a howling.

Storm was squirming in Annie's arms, he was whimpering, and Sandy called out, 'Water! It's water! It's into my shoes.'

'Back!' shouted Annie. 'Quick! Sandy, come on!'

Quick was not quick enough. The water rushing down the tunnel rose much more rapidly than the young flood tide pouring over the flat sands beyond the saltmarsh. Before Annie had taken more than half-a-dozen steps, it came over the top of her Wellingtons.

Storm began to wail.

'It's all right!' panted Annie. 'It's all right, Storm.'

But Storm sensed Annie's fear. He clung to her like a burr and would not be consoled.

'Sandy!' Annie could hear herself shouting. 'Lift your feet right out of the water. Don't wade. No, don't wade!'

But then Sandy lost his footing. He stumbled, and fell flat on his face, and dropped the torch. It went sailing away on the clear water, far beyond reach.

'You idiot!' screamed Annie. 'Come on!'

Sandy was choking; Annie was gasping.

121

'I can't swim,' he spluttered.

'Hold on to me,' bellowed Annie.

The cold water gripped Annie and Sandy by their waists. It crept up their ribcages. Under their armpits. It lifted them off their feet, and gently bounced them on the earthen floor.

'The ring!' cried Annie. 'That ring in the roof. It's our only chance.'

In her arms, Storm was shrieking. Shrieking and shuddering.

'Sandy!' gasped Annie. 'Hold on to me!'

The water rose even higher. Twice it bumped Annie's head against the stone roof and then, in the pallid light coming down the steps from the church, in the rush-and-gush-and-swarm-and-whistle of the water, Annie saw the iron ring.

With her right hand she was holding Storm, and Sandy was holding on to her belt, but with her left hand, Annie reached up and grabbed the ring. She knew their three lives depended on it.

'Storm!' she gasped. 'On to the step! Go on!'

Swinging from the ring by her left hand, Annie used her right hand, her right thigh and knee, to propel Storm towards the stone step. Then she summoned up all her strength and gave him a great push with her right foot. Storm fell face forward on to the dry step.

'Now you!' gasped Annie. 'Go on!'

Sandy was coughing and choking.

'Go on!' yelled Annie.

Still hanging on to Annie's belt with one hand, Sandy tried his utmost to wade across the current but it was too strong.

'I can't hold on!' screamed Annie.

Then Annie swung round to face Sandy. She

grabbed his right hand, she crowded him, and with her two legs she steered him and pushed towards the stone step. Up on to the step. On top of howling Storm.

'My hand!' gasped Annie. 'Don't let go!'

'I won't.'

'Pull me, can you?'

'Yes! Yes, I've got you! Let go!'

'I'm afraid.'

'Let go! You've got to. It's getting higher.'

'I'm letting go,' cried Annie.

Then Annie screwed up her eyes and let go of the iron ring. The racing, cold, clear water closed over her head.

Sandy held fast. He did not let Annie go. He held her hand fast, and slowly he hauled her out of the hungry torrent up on to the stone step.

In the gloom, the two of them crawled up a couple more steps well out of the reach of the yapping flood, but neither had the energy to climb right back into the church. Annie and Sandy knew how close they had come to being drowned, and for a time they and Storm lay there in a sodden heap, gasping and shaking, saying nothing.

'Up,' appealed a small voice. And again, a while later, 'Up.'

'Yes,' whispered Annie. 'Up. Come on.'

When she got to her feet, Annie wondered whether her legs were strong enough to support her. She felt as if all her bones had turned to jelly.

'That ring . . .' she said in a low voice. She rubbed her eyes.

'I know.'

'If we'd been carried downstream . . .'

'I know,' Sandy said again.

'If we'd gone left instead of right . . . We could never have waded back. The water's still rising. Soon there won't even be breathing space.'

Sandy levered himself on to his hands and knees. Then he stood up. 'All this for nothing,' he said, and he sounded tetchy.

'What do you mean?'

'We were nearly waterslain, and what have we learned?'

'We tried.'

'Any angels down here would have been washed out years ago. Swept away.'

'Like we were,' Annie replied, 'very nearly.'

'All three of us,' snapped Sandy. ' "They're hiding in the tunnel. They're waiting for us." That's what you said.'

Up in the church again, Storm's teeth began to chatter, so Annie wrapped the scruffy rug round him. Then she and Sandy quickly replaced the loose tiles over the trapdoor.

Sandy shuddered and shook his head. 'Death-trap,' he said.

'I've got to get home before Willa and my parents.'

'Sorry about the flashlight,' volunteered Sandy.

'That nearly did for us,' Annie said darkly.

'I tripped.'

'How am I meant to explain?'

'Say you were moth-catching,' Sandy suggested. 'Last night.'

'Moths have got more sense than to go out in the rain,' Annie replied.

'We're not going to get beat,' said Sandy. 'Not by Leppard or anyone else.'

'We may be too late already.'

'No,' said Sandy fiercely. 'If they're still here, we're going to find them.'

Annie gently removed Storm's rug wrapping. 'Upsy-daisy!' she said. 'Yes, we're going to find them. We are, aren't we, angel?'

18

'If the rain goes on like this,' Annie told Storm, 'we'll have to build an ark. Like Mr and Mrs Noah.'

'Noser ark,' said Storm.

'Exactly,' agreed Annie. 'Our cottage looks like a boat. Out at sea. Now, Storm, remember. Sshh! Say nothing.'

Storm looked at Annie with such a serious face. 'Nothing,' he agreed in his piping voice.

Quickly Annie dressed him in a dry pair of shorts and a fresh singlet, and then she changed her own clothes.

'When they get home, I'll say we went out on the marsh and then the rain lashed down,' Annie rehearsed. 'And I haven't put our clothes on the line because it's still raining.'

Then Annie saw it was already one o'clock, so she made two pieces of toast and warmed up a can of baked beans. As soon as Storm had finished, he started to suck his thumb and his eyes began to glaze.

'I know,' said Annie. 'I'm tired too.' Tenderly she laid Storm on the settee, and then she trudged up the little wooden staircase to her bedroom.

Lying on her bed, Annie heard her father telling her that, likely as not, the Ghost Beck would burst. She heard the grumbling and growling, the roaring and howling. Then her left hand began to burn, as if she'd scorched it on the top of the Aga cooker . . . She fell asleep.

In her dream Annie saw the angels again. They

were all wading along a marsh creek in the dark. Their golden eyes were torches and they were wearing Wellingtons. Moths were flickering and fluttering around their shining haloes. Then one angel coughed and raised his oily fingers as if he had something important to say.

'Leppard!' exclaimed Annie. 'I never even knew you were an angel.'

The angel Leppard coughed again, he cleared his throat loudly, and Annie opened her eyes.

At once she heard the gasp-and-splutter of the Hillman outside, and then she heard her mother's voice. She jumped up.

Annie met her mother and Willa at the door.

'You look as if you've been asleep,' her mother said.

'I have,' said Annie. 'Storm has too.'

'That's not like you.'

'Look at him!' said Willa, dropping on to her knees beside the settee.

'He's been an angel,' Annie told her.

Mrs Carter looked at Annie suspiciously. 'Is that so?' she said.

'I thought the day was drying up and so we went out on the marsh, and then the rain lashed down. We got soaked, absolutely soaked.'

'You wait till you hear what your father has to say,' Mrs Carter told her in a very dry voice.

'And so I changed Storm as soon as we got back,' Annie went on, 'into a dry pair of shorts and a fresh singlet, and then I changed too.' She knew she was talking too much, but somehow she couldn't stop herself. 'And after that I made us baked beans on toast. And after that . . .'

Mr Carter swung in through the door on his two

sticks. 'Have you told Annie?' he boomed.

'What?' asked Annie in a nervous voice.

'We stopped at the post office and there was quite a crowd. Blast! That's like I said. The old Ghost Beck has broken cover.'

'Really?' exclaimed Annie. She felt breathless.

'First time for seven years. That's run through the cellars all down the village street.'

'High as my hips,' said Willa.

'Higher,' said Mr Carter, 'and still rising. High as your head, Annie.'

'And that, young lady,' Annie's mother added, 'that's exactly why I warned you not to go round the church again. As I told you, the tunnel . . .'

'Five feet high,' Mr Carter interrupted.

'. . . the Ghost Beck runs through it.'

'That'll feed all the wells,' Mr Carter went on, 'but that's all it's good for. Blast!'

The sheer force of Mr Carter's voice woke Storm up. He gazed at his mother and sucked his right thumb.

Willa ran her fingers through his curly dark brown hair and, behind her, Annie gave Storm a frozen, warning look.

Storm pulled his thumb out of his mouth and squashed his nose with his forefinger. 'Sshh!' he whispered.

'Did you go out on the marsh then?' his mother asked him.

'Nothing!' murmured Storm. And with that, he fell asleep again.

'What's been going on?' Mrs Carter asked.

Annie shrugged. 'Nothing,' she said.

'The Reverend came in to the post office,' Mr Carter went on. 'Quite a crowd there was. He said he knows we aren't church people, but he's inviting us anyhow. He's got an important announcement.'

Annie frowned. 'What kind of announcement?' she asked in an accusing voice.

'How would I know?' her mother replied.

'Little Miss Suspicious,' said Willa, smiling. 'Actually, the Reverend did say he thought you would be especially interested.'

'Especially pleased.' Mrs Carter corrected her. 'That's what he said.'

'Especially pleased?' Annie repeated. 'Why me?'

But Annie knew the answer to her own question. Leppard must have beaten her and Sandy to it, and found the angels.

'Ten o'clock tomorrow,' Mr Carter said.

*   *   *

The Reverend Potter stood in front of the altar. He beamed. He nodded. This was his big moment, and he wasn't going to hurry.

'Welcome!' he said in a loud voice. And then, more slowly, 'Well come to God's house. Packed like sardines! I haven't seen the church this full for years, not even at Christmas or Easter. Old faces. New faces.' The rector inclined his head towards Sandy and Gracie. ' 'Slainers. Furriners. Little ones too. Angel-faces.'

'Little devils, reverend,' a woman's voice called out at the back of the church.

A lot of people turned round, and almost everyone laughed.

'Trust Gracie!' Margie Carter said to her

129

husband in a hoarse voice. 'Never can keep her big mouth shut.'

'Now this is no regular church service,' the Reverend Potter continued, 'but let's begin with a sing-song. I think we should, don't you?'

The rector peered at the little scoreboard lashed to a pillar in the nave.

'Hymn four hundred and fifteen,' he announced.

'Four hundred and seventy-five,' a voice corrected him.

'What?'

'Four hundred and seventy-five, reverend.'

The Reverend Potter peered at the scoreboard again, and his right eyebrow jerked up and down. 'Ah, yes,' he said. 'I do declare.'

'How many for, reverend?' another voice called out.

Everyone laughed again.

'4–7–5,' the rector said. 'Ye holy angels bright . . . assist our song. And while you're at it,' he added cheerfully, 'assist my sight too.'

I knew it, thought Annie. I knew this was going to be about the angels.

During the hymn, Annie turned round once and looked across the nave at Sandy. He wasn't singing. He was staring at the wall with the three broken tablets and the scratched inscription:

Between her Will
And his Wall
Waterslain
We Lie Waiting

You said you were waiting, waiting for me,

130

Annie thought. In my dream, you did. When you gave me that piece of honeycomb and put your cool hand on my forehead. Annie felt so confused.

During the last verse of the hymn, the Reverend Potter climbed into the pretty wine-glass pulpit. It looked altogether too delicate to withstand such a big man.

The rector raised his eyes to heaven—and the missing angels. 'May the words of my mouth,' he boomed, 'be acceptable, O Lord, in Thy sight.' He smiled at his congregation. 'Now do sit down everyone. Make yourselves comfortable.'

Shuffling. Scraping. Coughing. At last there was something like silence.

At least, there would have been. But at this moment Storm announced, clear as a bell, 'Sshh! Say nothing!'

Everyone laughed. Everyone except Willa.

'Storm!' she said in a stifled voice. 'Smack.'

Storm shook his head and wriggled.

'Yes,' said the Reverend Potter with a smile. 'Say nothing! As often as not, that's good advice. But on this occasion, I've something important to tell you.' The rector paused, and nodded first to Sandy and then to Annie. 'Not so long ago, I met my young friends, Annie Carter and Sandy Boroff, out on the marsh. Sandy was splattered with mud and I told him he looked like a dark angel. And do you know what Annie said? Right out, she asked me, "What is an angel?"'

'You've seen the exhibition in the village hall,' the rector went on. 'Well, most of you have. Our beautiful wing. The one Alan Leppard found in the Rectory attic. And you all know . . .' The Reverend Potter tilted back his almost hairless head and waved at the roof. '. . . you all know our angels are missing.

'I'm not a thinker,' the Reverend Potter continued. 'I'm a doer. Some people think you won't see God unless you're on your knees. I don't think that. I've seen Him while out sailing. But Annie's question, it's a tough one, and it has made me think.

'What I told Annie and Sandy,' the rector went on, 'is that angels are supermen and superwomen. They carry messages from God to human beings. You know, like the angel Gabriel and the Virgin Mary. That's right, isn't it, Annie?'

Annie looked at Pitterpatter, unblinking. You told us about dark angels, she thought. And in my dream you were a dark angel yourself, wrecking our church.

'Let me tell you a little story,' said the Reverend Potter. 'There was once a pope called Gregory. One day, wandering through the market-place in Rome, he saw some boys for sale. Yes,' said the rector, shaking his head, 'they were wearing manacles and leg-irons and a trader was selling them. Selling them as slaves. These boys had fair skin and fair reddish hair—a bit like mine before I lost it—and chiselled features.'

He means John Chisel, thought Annie.

'Good cheekbones,' said the rector. 'You know.'

'"Where do these boys come from?" Pope Gregory asked.

'"The island of Britain," the trader replied. "Most people look like that up there"

'"Are they Christian?" asked the pope.

'"Never!" said the trader. "They're all heathens. They worship idols."

132

'Pope Gregory sighed. "Such handsome boys," he said, "but with such ugly minds. What are they called?"

'"Angles," the trader told him.

'"Quite right," said Pope Gregory. "Angles. These boys do have angelic faces. If only they could all become one with the angels . . ." And then,' the Reverend Potter continued, 'Pope Gregory sent Saint Augustine and a team of missionaries here to Britain, and England—Angle-land, that's to say—became Christian.'

Annie turned round and sneaked another look at Sandy, but he was still staring at the wall with the inscription on it.

'So why am I telling you this?' the Reverend Potter asked.

Yes, thought Annie. Why?

'Appearances aren't enough,' the rector answered himself. 'It's not enough to look handsome, or pretty, or beautiful. It's not enough to look like angels. We must find the angel-part in each of us, the part that always knows what's good and right and true.'

The rector shook his head. 'But we're only human,' he said. 'We've all got failings and we all think ugly thoughts from time to time. We need help. We need our own Waterslain angels to guide us.'

Annie twisted round to look at Sandy again, and out of the corner of one eye, she saw Alan Leppard with his wife and Geraldine and her younger brother sitting in the pew behind Sandy and Gracie. Alan was looking straight at her, his mouth hanging open as if he were smoking a fag, slightly smiling.

He's scoffing at me, thought Annie.

'Turn round!' Mrs Carter hissed. 'What do you think you are doing?'

You crook. You know where they are. You've already found them.

'And so I come at last to my announcement,' said the Reverend Potter. 'As you know, our angels are missing. They are lost . . . and I can't say I think they'll ever be found again. As it happens,' said the rector, 'I don't really believe they were destroyed during the Reformation or in Cromwell's time, when so many church paintings and sculptures hereabouts were smashed to pieces. No, I believe they're around here somewhere . . .'

And you were searching for them, thought Annie. You were, weren't you, when we met you on the marsh and you were carrying that long pole.

'. . . and I know I'm not the only one.' The rector gazed straight at Annie. 'But where?' he asked. 'Where are they? I've honestly got no idea.

'Now then!' said Pitterpatter. 'I've been talking to our treasurer and we actually have a fair bit in the kitty. Enough even to think about replacing our angels.'

Replacing! Annie frowned. How can you replace them?

'With fibreglass copies,' Pitterpatter explained. 'Advanced technology! Fibreglass angels, and we'll paint them the original colours.'

Annie narrowed her eyes. What's going on? I bet you know where they are, you as well as Leppard. Are you in league with him? Are you going to sell them into slavery?

'We'll use what church funds we have,' the Reverend Potter went on, 'and we'll launch a

134

public appeal. To get things started, my wife and I have decided to give one hundred pounds of our own money.'

Annie sat bolt upright, and very still. She realised she was shivering.

Our angels. Our quest. Our beautiful Waterslain angels.

Annie gave a great sob.

Mrs Carter looked at her daughter, startled. Gently, she put her right arm around her.

Annie couldn't help herself. She didn't make another sound, but hot tears streamed down her cold cheeks.

'Naturally,' said the Reverend Potter, 'we hope everyone here can give a bob or two. Whether or not you're churchgoers, our angels are part of your story. They lived here. Yes, they lived here once, just like you do now. So now, let's round things off with another hymn. Hymn 336. That's right, isn't it?'

'Yes,' assented a dozen voices.

'Hymn 336,' the Reverend Potter repeated. 'Angel-voices ever singing . . . angel-harps for ever ringing.'

Annie rubbed her eyes and cheeks with the back of her hand, and for a third time she turned round to look at Sandy. He was looking straight at her, and behind his thick-rimmed spectacles his dark eyes were dilated.

Annie knew at once he needed to say something to her, something urgent, something crucial.

Sandy pointed to his watch. Slowly he raised two fingers.

19

What can I do, thought Annie. How can I find out whether Leppard's beaten us? Is he about to sell them?

Holding Storm's chubby left hand, she walked down the muddy path leading from their little cottage garden straight into the marsh.

'Carry,' Storm suggested, more in hope than expectation.

'No,' said Annie. 'Walk first, then carry.'

But almost at once Annie relented, because the nettles on either side of the path were hip-high and, for Storm, head-high. She hoisted him on to her shoulders, and Storm laughed for joy, and far above them, halfway to heaven, the larks sang descants.

Beside the old twisted willow, Annie set Storm on his feet again.

How, thought Annie. How can we stop him? Shall I ring Josie Sidebottom again? No, what good would that be?

Out into the wilderness of the marsh Annie walked, and Storm trailed behind her.

I could talk to Miss McQueen, I could. She's very clever and she keeps herself to herself. She might be able to help me.

I know. I'll go back to Baker's in Fakenham. Where Alan was selling that little angel. He may have said something to the manager. About soon having more angels for sale. Something like that.

'Carry,' said a plaintive voice.

People always leave clues, thought Annie. Dad

says the truth will always out, and that's why there's no such thing as a perfect murder.

Annie squatted beside a little marsh pool, and Storm knelt down next to her. He almost tucked himself into her. The pool was shaped like a saucer, fringed with bristly grass, and the clear salty water was tepid.

'Look!' said Annie. 'Shrimps! Can you see them?'

Storm cried out in delight. He bent forward until he almost fell into his reflection.

The transparent shrimps scooted and squirted round and round the little pool.

Round and round, thought Annie. Round and round. That's all I'm doing. Going round and round and not getting anywhere.

What did Josie Sidebottom say when we met her? 'You're fishing in deep waters.'

'Be careful,' she said. Why?

Annie sighed and remembered Sandy's signal. Two o'clock, she thought. At least, I think that's what he meant. I've got to talk to him.

A deep rib of shadow crossed the marsh. The wind rode in front of it, and the little pool darkened and shivered.

'Come on, Storm,' said Annie. 'We'd better be getting home.'

As soon as Annie got to her feet, Storm reached out, and Annie settled him on her shoulders. And on their way back, Annie and Storm put up a redshank from a deep, muddy creek.

'See it?' cried Annie. 'Its long bill. Lovely orange-red.'

Away flew the redshank, yelping, warning all the other birds that Annie was on her way.

'Noisy thing!' remarked Annie.

'Teuk, teuk, teuk!' the redshank scolded her.

I'll stalk you, thought Annie. I'll snare you. I'll save you. I won't let you get away.

*   *   *

When Annie reached the church, Sandy was already there, and he wasn't nesting in the pulpit. He was standing beside the cracked tablets and the scratched inscription on the south wall.

'Annie!' he called out. 'I've been here forever.'

'I was as quick as I could. There's five at home, and Willa never stops talking, and I had to read to Storm after dinner until he got sleepy.'

'OK,' said Sandy. 'Keep your hair on.'

Annie was so used to Sandy looking pale-skinned and even half-transparent that she was quite startled to see him so flushed.

'Are you all right?' she asked him.

By way of reply, Sandy turned back to the south wall.

'I saw you staring at something,' said Annie. 'You know, while Pitterpatter was talking. Oh, Sandy! What are we going to do? We got so near. So near I thought I could feel the air fanned by their wings. And now Leppard has beaten us. He's found our angels, and he's going to sell them into slavery.'

'No, Annie,' said Sandy in a low voice.

'No, what?'

'Leppard hasn't found them. I don't think he has. Not in the tunnel anyway.'

'He has!' cried Annie. 'I'm sure he has. You know how he tried to stop us going down into the

138

tunnel.'

'Even so.'

'Did you believe Pitterpatter when he said our angels would never be found?'

'Kinda. Look at these letters, Annie. Now the sun's come out, they've come out as well!'

Between her Will
And his Wall
Waterslain
We Lie Waiting

'Why didn't we bother about the first two lines?' Sandy said.

'Before, you mean,' said Annie. 'I don't know. I said it didn't matter.'

'Yeah, well . . . maybe it does.'

'Go on, then,' said Annie. 'You've found out something. I can tell you have.'

Sandy gleamed. 'OK. "Waterslain We Lie Waiting". Who's doing the talking?'

'What do you mean?'

'Who's "we"?'

'Well . . . the angels.'

'Yup. So the angels are telling us how they're drowned, and how they're lying down, and how they're waiting. But in the first two lines, aren't they also telling us where they are?'

'Between her Will and his Wall,' Annie replied.

Sandy stuck his tongue out a bit. 'Whose wall?' he asked.

'I don't know,' said Annie. 'His.'

'His,' said Sandy. 'His. Whose? We gotta find out. What about "her Will"?'

Annie shook her head. 'Someone who's made

139

one,' she faltered.

Sandy gave Annie a crafty, sideways look.

'Oh!' cried Annie. 'I get it! Will. William.'

The corners of Sandy's mouth twitched. 'And if so . . .' he went on slowly, not taking his eyes off the wall.

Annie yelped. 'This tablet. The one we looked at before. Will . . . Will . . . someone. 1642. Erected by his wife Tabitha.'

Sandy turned to Annie and stared at her, unblinking.

'You mean, between this tablet and . . . his Wall . . . You're brilliant, Sandy!'

Sandy stuck out his lower lip. 'Blame Father Gabriel!' he said.

'But you said these tablets weren't clues. You said they were just memorials.'

'So I messed up too,' Sandy replied.

' "His Wall," ' said Annie. 'Whose wall?'

'That's the question,' Sandy said. 'Not the church ones, anyhow. They're not thick enough for angels to hide inside.'

'The wall round the churchyard, then?'

'In which case our angels are buried somewhere in the graveyard.'

Annie clicked her tongue and shook her head.

'We can't start digging people up,' said Sandy.

'Oh!' exclaimed Annie. 'What about the Rectory? That's old. It's medieval.' She pointed out of the little leaded window. 'What if they're in the Rectory garden?'

' "His Wall," ' mused Sandy. 'The minister's— well, the rector's wall. That adds up. The rector back then might have heard that Smasher's men were coming and decided to hide the angels. Let's have a look.'

'There's a door in the vestry,' Annie told him. 'Sandy, my heart's beating.'

'I hope so!' said Sandy.

'You know what I mean.'

'My eyeballs are burning.'

'Come on!' Annie urged him.

What wind there was blew from the north-west, and the church stood up to it as it had done for centuries. Sometimes, when the wind put its mouth to the salt-eaten limestone, the church whistled softly, sometimes it shuddered like a fishing smack caught broadside by a rearing dark wave. But for most of the time it rose silent and enduring. And for most of the people in the village, the church was their occasional meeting-place, witness to their loving and their grieving, and it was their door out of this world.

In the shelter of the church, the southern corner of the churchyard was very still. Even the big conker tree stood silently to attention. And beyond the decrepit little gate in the crumbling churchyard wall, the Rectory garden was waiting for them.

'It feels so ancient here,' Sandy said in a quiet voice.

'You always say that,' Annie replied. 'It feels so neglected.'

'Sort of shaggy.'

'I hope the rector and Mrs aren't at home,' said Sandy.

'I know,' Annie agreed. 'If they come out, we'll just have to make something up.'

'OK,' said Sandy. 'Between her Will and his Wall . . . So which wall?'

'I don't know. The one facing the church, I

suppose.'

Annie and Sandy gazed at the grey Rectory wall. It had three windows. A fourth one had been blocked up. A pointed arch was built into the wall, and beneath it was a long door—or that's what it looked like. And up at the top, under the lead gutter, there was a ragged row of grey stone tablets.

'They look like a row of broken teeth,' said Sandy.

'This wall's really ancient,' Annie said. 'It could have been built long before the angels were hidden.'

'Even if it's the right one . . .' Sandy kept blinking in a worried way. 'Even if it is . . .'

'I know,' agreed Annie. 'It's twenty or thirty yards to the churchyard wall, and the same from there to the church.'

'We gotta make a start somewhere,' Sandy said. 'Let's make a straight line from the tablet on the church wall to the nearest point of the Rectory wall.'

'What with?'

'You got some string?'

'No,' said Annie. 'Only a tincey bit.'

'Stones, then,' said Sandy. 'Or sticks. Let's mark out a line from Will to Wall.'

'What's the point?'

'Like I said, we gotta get started. We can't dig the whole joint up.'

'You keep having ideas,' said Annie, 'but all we're doing is going round and round, like shrimps in a mud pool.'

'So do you,' Sandy objected. 'You keep having ideas as well. Up the tower, and what happened?

We got stung. Down the tunnel, what happened? We nearly got drowned.'

'And you dropped the torch.'

'And if you're so sure Leppard's found the angels, why are you still looking for them?'

'Only because of you!' Annie protested loudly. 'Only because you think you're so clever.'

'We're not getting anywhere like this,' said Sandy. He took off his specs, and Annie saw they'd all furred up.

Annie clicked her tongue noisily. Then she began to pick up sticks for markers. And when Sandy had carefully rubbed the inside of each lens on his sleeve, he helped her.

Crouching in the lank grass, there was a hunk of grey-white stone, large as a beer barrel; and on the stone, a pigeon was lying on its back in a soft bed of its own loose, silvery-grey feathers. Its stomach had been ripped open and the stone was spattered with blood.

Sandy made a choking noise.

'It's like a sacrifice,' said Annie in a low voice.

'A sacrifice to the great god Owl,' Sandy added. 'Look! The stone's dressed.'

'What do you mean?'

'It's been chiselled and carved. It's part of a pillar or something.'

'You know so many words,' said Annie.

'Because of Father Gabriel,' Sandy replied, and he started to prowl around the damp grey-green garden. 'There's another one over here,' he called out.

'Sshh! Pitterpatter might hear.'

'In fact . . . this whole flowerbed's lined with bits of carved stone.'

143

Annie walked over to have a look. 'Not faces, though,' she said. 'Not angels.'

'This garden's a bit of a dump, really,' Sandy observed. 'Tangles and weeds.' He walked up to the enormous tree in the middle of the lawn.

'Weeping willow,' said Annie.

'Weeping? Why?'

'I don't know. Because all its branches are bending down.'

'Right down to the ground,' said Sandy. 'My mom's got a long green skirt that comes down to the ground.'

He separated the willow curtain and stepped in, and Annie followed him.

'It's like we're in a green tent or something,' Annie said.

Sandy kicked at a massive stump quite close to the trunk of the willow, below a thick branch. Then he bent down and pulled at the dusty strings of ivy strangling it.

'Hey!' he said. 'This isn't a tree stump.'

Sandy unhitched a bit more of the ivy, until he and Annie could see a circle of very small purplish-brown bricks. They came up to Annie's and Sandy's shins, and were topped with a rotten wooden lid.

'It's a well,' said Annie in a hoarse voice.

'I know,' Sandy replied. 'This bit—above ground—it's called the coping.'

'I know that, you dud. We've got one. Dad put the old windlass and bucket into the display.'

Sandy prodded at the edge of the wooden lid with his right toe, and several woodlice and a bronze centipede scurried for cover in the ivy. 'No one's been near this one for ages,' he said.

144

'Let's get the lid off.'

'It'll fall apart,' said Sandy. He took a step back. Then another.

'What are you doing?'

Sandy looked at Annie, and behind his spectacles his grey eyes were gleaming. He stuck the tip of his tongue between his lips.

'What is it?'

'Our Father, which art in heaven,' Sandy said, and he couldn't stop smiling. 'I got it! Annie, I got it. It was under our noses the whole time, it's just we never saw it.'

'What?'

Sandy pretended to be a cockerel. First he stalked round the well slapping down one foot, then the other, and then he threw back his head and crowed. He crowed!

'Sandy!' cried Annie, as alarmed as she was excited. 'Sshh!'

Sandy flapped his arms. 'Between her Will . . .' he began. 'Between her Will . . .'

'. . . and his Wall,' continued Annie.

'Yeah. What comes between will and wall?'

'What do you mean?'

'Between will and wall,' Sandy repeated, 'wall and will.'

'What does?' faltered Annie. 'I don't know.'

'You do.'

Annie slowly shook her head.

'Between a and i,' said Sandy in a steady voice.

'Oh!' cried Annie. 'E! E does.'

'Got it!' said Sandy.

'Well! Well comes between wall and will.'

Sandy threw back his head and laughed.

'Brilliant!' exclaimed Annie. 'You're brilliant.

I'd never have thought of that. Never, never. My legs are all shaky.'

'Journey's end,' said Sandy. 'Gratias deo.'

'What?'

'Thanks be to God.'

'This is where they are,' Annie said. 'It is, isn't it.'

'Must be,' said Sandy.

'Waterslain and waiting,' Annie said.

Annie and Sandy stood facing each other across the well. Together they grasped the lid and tried to slide it off the top of the coping, but the soggy wood just crumbled in their hands.

'All right,' said Annie. 'We'll have to take it off handful by handful. Don't let too much fall in.'

'Pitterpatter will notice. Him or Mrs.'

'It can't be helped,' said Annie. 'It's too late now. Anyhow, I bet they haven't been here in hundreds of years.'

Kneeling on either side of the coping, Annie and Sandy stared down into the dark.

A ghastly stink rose up and wound itself around them, the stench of rotting plants and rancid small jobs and sludgy big jobs. They could taste it in their throats. It half-suffocated them.

Sandy coughed noisily.

'How deep is it?' whispered Annie. 'Oh, I know!' She dug a pebble out of the earth with her fingertips. 'I'll drop this in.'

After Annie had dropped the pebble into the well, she heard her heart thump three times, and then—cluck!

'Do it again,' said Sandy.

Annie prised another pebble out of the earth under the willow, and dropped it into the well.

146

Cluck!

'It sounds like airholes in the mud,' Annie said, 'you know, popping when the tide's coming in.'

'Two and a half seconds,' said Sandy. 'That's, er, that's about fifty feet.'

'Fifty!'

'Or sixty.'

'How do you know?'

'Science class,' said Sandy. 'My extra one, with Father Gabriel.'

'That's longer than the ladder in the church.'

'Twice as long.'

The two of them leaned over the coping again.

'Is that what I think it is?' Sandy asked. He pointed to the plant growing out of the side of the wall, about six feet down. 'Under that fern.'

'I can't tell,' said Annie, and she ran across the garden to the nearest flowerbed and came back with a stake, and poked at the fern.

'It's a rung,' she exclaimed. 'Look! There's another one below it.'

'Yeah.'

'And a third one . . . I think there is.'

'And below that,' said Sandy, in a mournful voice, 'nothing but the dark. Down and down into the depths, into the dark and the drowning.'

'Sandy!' protested Annie.

'And everything else beginning with D.'

'Are they safe, do you think? I mean . . . how long ago . . .' Annie's voice tailed off, but the well caught her words and rolled them round its open, dark mouth. 'I'll give it a try,' she went on. 'I'll have to.'

'I could, if you want,' said Sandy in a flat voice.

Annie shook her head.

'You'll be better than me.'

'I'll give it a try,' Annie said again.

'Attagirl!' said Sandy, admiringly.

'I know. We've got some rope at home. I'll tie it round me . . .'

'. . . and I'll hold the other end,' Sandy added.

'No,' said Annie. 'That's no good. If a rung comes loose, I mean, if it comes out of the wall, I'll drag you down. We can throw the rope over this big branch above the well. It's perfect, very round and smooth. And you'll have to pay it out.'

'Up and down,' said Sandy. 'And now down again. Norfolk's not flat. It's all towers and tunnels and wells.'

'We'll have to wait until after evensong,' Annie told him. 'Half-past six. After that, the warden locks up the church, and there won't be anyone about.'

'And Storm will be in bed,' Sandy added. 'We can't have him up here.'

'No,' agreed Annie. 'It's too dangerous.'

In the quiet of the scruffy garden, Annie and Sandy could hear the pigeons gulping and the blackbirds warning and, far overhead, the skylarks bubbling. They could hear the sound of their own warm breathing. They could almost hear the silence of the waiting well.

'Annie,' began Sandy, but then he frowned and clicked his tongue.

'What?'

'Well . . . we never talk about anything.'

'We do.'

Sandy stared at Annie.

'You told me about your dad. Disappearing and everything.'

'Yeah,' said Sandy, unconvinced.

'What's wrong?'

'Well, what is it between your mom and mine?'

'That!' exclaimed Annie. 'I don't know exactly.'

'Mom says yours wants to drive her out. Right out of Waterslain.'

'Never,' said Annie.

'Well, my mom thinks she does.'

'It's just the way she talks,' said Annie.

Sandy slowly shook his head.

'I did hear them arguing,' Annie said. 'My mum and dad, down in the kitchen. They thought I was asleep. About how my dad used to fancy your mum, and how my mum knows he still does. And my dad said he doesn't, but my mum said she can tell from the way he looks at her.'

'That adds up,' said Sandy. 'My mom told me your dad asked her to marry him, and she said yes, but then my dad came along.'

'Wow!' said Annie.

'So your mom was his second choice,' Sandy said. 'Maybe she sort-of thinks she's still second best.'

'She's older than Dad,' Annie explained. 'And she'd been married before. Her first husband— well, he left her. He just walked away. That's what Dad told me.'

'Right,' said Sandy, slowly.

'So Willa's only my half-sister. She's twelve years older than me.'

'OK.'

'If you ask me,' said Annie, 'it's a good thing your dad did come along. Otherwise, you and I wouldn't exist.'

'I used to wonder if I did,' said Sandy in a glum

149

voice.

'Did what?'

'Exist. Hidden away the whole time. Mom always made me stay in. She said I was too sickly to mix with other people because I might catch polio or something.'

'What about school, though?'

'It was a Catholic school. Pretty normal. I had lots of extra lessons from Father Gabriel. He told me he wanted me to fall in love with words. Especially the ones in the Bible! I miss him, he was a kind of dad.'

'Our school's pretty normal too,' said Annie.

'But . . . well . . . will I fit in?'

'Why not?'

'Mom says Norfolk kids are tough. She says there's bullying.'

'You'll be OK,' said Annie. 'There's lots of boys in Waterslain who are even weirder than you.'

Sandy nodded and laid two old stakes over the top of the well. 'I haven't ever talked so much to someone my own age,' he told Annie. 'There's lots we could talk about.'

*   *   *

'Are you off your trolley?' Mrs Carter demanded. 'Haven't you forgotten something?'

'What?' asked Annie.

'It's Willa's and Storm's last night here.'

'But I promised, Mum.'

'Hang Sandy!' exclaimed Mrs Carter. 'He can wait. There's no question of your going out after dinner.'

'Mum!'

'He'll be here tomorrow, won't he?'

'I'd forgotten.'

'And now I've reminded you.'

So half-past six came and went and Annie was unable to meet Sandy and, because he and his mum hadn't got a telephone, she couldn't even tell him. Instead, she played tiddlywinks with Storm, and then she read him a story in bed.

'More,' said Storm, sucking his thumb.

Annie hugged Storm. 'Next time.'

Then Annie sat down to eat with her parents and Willa—roast chicken, like they always had on last evenings, and a glass of sweet white wine from the bottle Mr Carter kept at the back of the corner cupboard.

'Half a glass and that goes straight to my head,' giggled Willa.

'Can I have a sip?' asked Annie.

Her parents ignored her.

'Can I?'

'Don't be so silly,' said Mrs Carter.

'Diluted,' Annie suggested.

'No,' said her father.

'Willa,' Annie began, 'when's Rod coming home?'

Willa sighed and shook her head. 'He's back in the Indian Ocean,' she replied. 'In five weeks, he says. I miss him, I really do.'

'I do too,' said Annie.

After supper the four of them played cards. And then Willa and Mrs Carter chatted while Mr Carter read the *News and Advertiser*. And all the while, Annie kept thinking about the black mouth of the well, and wondering whether the rungs would be safe, and whether the angels would be

151

there, and not being able to meet Sandy, and what he would suppose.

'She's got her head in the clouds, your young sister,' Mrs Carter observed.

'So I see,' said Willa.

'Up amongst the angels,' Mrs Carter said, shaking her head. 'We don't know half what's been going on.'

'Probably just as well,' Willa said. 'Isn't it, sister?'

'What?' asked Annie.

Mrs Carter snorted.

'Little Annie head-in-air,' said Willa, smiling, 'her dad's delight, her mum's despair. Eyes on the sky, toes in the mud. Angels singing in her blood.'

Annie looked at Willa, astonished. 'Did you make that up?' she asked.

20

Not long after Annie tramped up to her little bedroom she went out into the saltmarsh.

Full moon. No more than a few lamb clouds. The sky's immense dome, velvet, midnight blue. The sparkling stitches of thousands and thousands of stars. Annie took a deep breath. All around her, she could see sprigs of spiky sea-holly, no longer blue-green but ashen, twigs of samphire, ashen, the silver backs of sea-lavender leaves, the pale staring eyes of bindweed bells.

Somewhere out in the marsh, a colony of birds began to jostle and complain. And then to peep-peep-peep.

'Oyster-catchers,' Annie said to herself. 'As smart as they look. You won't catch them napping.'

Far off, very far off, Annie could hear voices. They were counting.

No, thought Annie, and you won't catch me. You won't. I know you're seeking me. I know you're all counting up to one hundred and if you find me, my angels and I will be lost forever. But this is my place, this saltmarsh. Where shall I hide?

A barn owl came gliding over Annie's head, so close that it scared her.

'Get away!' exclaimed Annie, waving her white arms. 'I'm not a shrew! Not a vole, or anything.'

The owl hooted.

Fifty, fifty-one, fifty-two, fifty-three . . .

At least my seekers can't see in the dark, Annie thought. At least they haven't got radar. A dot on the radar screen is called an angel. Sandy told me that.

'All the same . . .' Annie said to herself. 'All the same, this moonlight's so bright. Shining on my face, my white hands.'

Annie began to pick pieces of sea-lavender and, disturbed from its perch, a dozy insect began to thrum. Then it alighted on Annie's nose.

'Clear off!' Annie commanded it. 'You're not a bee, are you?'

Sixty-six, sixty-seven, sixty-eight . . .

Annie buried her face in her bundle of sea-lavender. Its perfume was sweet and yet slightly salty, thick and warm.

If anyone comes near, Annie thought . . .

Seventy-four, seventy-five, seventy-six . . .

. . . if anyone comes near, I'll bury my face in it. And I'll roll down the sleeves of my nightie and pull them over my hands. It's a good thing I'm wearing my navy blue one.

Eighty-eight, eighty-nine, ninety . . .

Annie ran down the marsh path to the mud hole and quickly dipped each of her feet into it, and then she spread black mud over her face and hands.

This is even better than sea-lavender, she thought. Better than my nightie.

Ninety-three, ninety-four . . .

Annie hurried along the string-thin path beside the Mill Fleet, she brushed through the purslane and sea-blite and the purple-yellow sea-aster, all of them ashen in the moonlight.

Ninety-seven, ninety-eight . . .

Then she threw herself face down into the coarse grass and it made way for her and couched her. So there she was, Annie, out in the middle of the saltmarsh in the middle of the night in this middle-world.

Ninety-nine . . .

Moon, thought Annie. I wish you'd hide your face too. You're too bright. Still, they'll never find me. I don't think they will.

The tide's sip and seep; mud-slurp; bird-chirp. But after a while it seemed to Annie that all the little night-sounds were holding their breath. She curled into herself, almost unborn again.

'One hun-dred!'

A circle of voices were calling out from all directions, some from the village, some from the dunes that stood between Annie and the rasping sea, some from below her, deep down in the marsh, some from the dark and winking well of the sky.

'One hun-dred. Dred! Dred! Ready or not, we're coming. We're coming, ready or not.'

Annie screwed up her eyes and saw her seekers. She saw them all. And she could hear each word they were saying.

Josie Sidebottom staggered over a sinking dune, gasping for breath.

'My word!' she gasped. 'Out here, old as I am. Still, I must warn her if it's the last thing I do. Annie! Annie! Where are you? You're fishing in deep waters.'

Then Annie saw Pitterpatter hurrying up the marsh path, carrying a long hooked pole. 'This is where I overtook them,' he said to himself loudly. 'On my way to Dead Man's Pool. Annie, where are you? I'm going to sell you, sell you into slavery.'

Then a burly dark figure strode towards Annie straight across the marsh, ignoring the winding paths, splashing through tepid pools, clambering down into muddy creeks and up out of them again, swiping with his cudgel at cord-grass and sea-lavender, and the shrubs of scratchy sea-blite.

This man was whispering to himself, whispering, whispering, and Annie couldn't make out a word he was saying. But all at once he growled, 'Get her! Get her!'

No, no, cried Annie inside her own head.

'Get her! Get her! Hack her into pieces.'

It's Smasher, cried Annie. It's Smasher himself. It must be. Annie buried her muddy face in her bunch of sea-lavender and screwed up her eyes. Shooting stars leaped and danced in front of her. Smithereens of light.

In her hiding-place, Annie waited and shivered. But then she heard a quite gentle voice, calling, 'Annie! Annie, where are you, dear? It's me. Miss McQueen. You can come out now, Annie.'

Annie gave a sob and peeked through the lavender. She could see her old teacher, peering over her half-glasses, carefully picking her way between the coarse marsh plants.

'It's me, dear. Where are you?'

Annie didn't dare move. She didn't dare show herself, not even to Miss McQueen. She lay absolutely still until her old teacher had passed by, heading towards the open sea.

This place isn't safe, thought Annie. Not half as safe as I imagined. I've got to find my angels before a seeker finds me. I've got to.

As soon as she was sure she was on her own again, Annie broke cover. She jumped up and hared back to the black mud hole. There, she took a deep breath and, putting her hands over her face, she stepped right in. Up to her waist. Her shoulders. Up to her neck.

Annie gasped.

That was when she saw Alan Leppard. He was weaving from side to side up the marsh path, as if he had caught Annie's scent and was tracking her. Twice, three times, he doubled back, then advanced on her again.

'Gotcha!' he growled in his deep voice. 'You little angel. You little fool! I know you're here or hereabouts.'

Annie pressed her face into the lavender-mask; mud covered the rest of her. Her breathing was shallow and jerky.

He'll hear me, she thought. My heart. He'll hear it thumping.

'Where are you?' demanded Leppard. He stopped and swivelled round, then stared straight at the mud hole. 'Rushing in where angels fear to tread.' His voice was rising. 'Listen to me. You won't come up again.'

For a second time, Annie screwed up her eyes, and shooting stars leaped and danced in front of her.

This was when Annie heard a sweet sshh-sshh gently rising, rising and cradling her. As if the lightest wind had got up and were stirring the marsh reeds. As if she were in a little boat, rocking, quite safe, far out at sea.

And then Annie heard a soft, high whistling—not in the least sharp, more like warbling—a sound she had heard before.

In the dark, Annie opened her sloe-black eyes. And there, right in front of her, was the long-fingered angel who had stood beside her bed after she'd been stung by fourteen bees.

The angel's wings were white and shining, almost glowing, like the sheets of wild honey Annie had seen in the tower-room.

'You can come out now,' it said.

Annie looked up from the mud hole.

The angel smiled a patient smile. 'Annie, we are waiting for you.' Its clear, sweet voice somehow bubbled like a lark, risen clean above itself. 'Waiting and watching over you.'

Then the angel helped Annie out of the mud hole. Annie shook herself like a dog, and the mud flew in all directions.

'Oh! Sorry!' she cried. 'Sorry!'

But the angel had disappeared. Where it had been, there was nothing but a shaft, a current almost, of light. Then that too faded. Annie was standing alone on the marsh path.

Annie took a deep, deep breath, and then let it all out again, as slowly as she could. Already the eastern sky had begun to turn pale—pale grey, primrose, grey-green. Around Annie, gulls and waders were beginning to bark and mew and squeak as if trying out which voices would best suit them. The marsh itself breathed and sucked, thick with secrets, always moving, always the same. And away over the dunes, laced and knotted with marram grass, the sea rumbled.

'Oh!' carolled Annie. 'This ghost-light. Nowhere on earth is as beautiful as this. Nowhere's half as beautiful. My Waterslain.'

In her bed, Annie shifted and turned towards the east. She opened her eyes, instantly awake, already knowing this was the most important morning of her life.

21

The morning bus disappeared round the corner, and Annie and her mother stopped waving.

Mrs Carter looked so deflated. 'That's that, then,' she said with a heartfelt sigh.

'You always say that,' Annie told her.

'I always wonder whether I'll ever see them again.'

Annie looked at her mother, startled. 'Course you will.'

'Life's so . . . chancy. Here one moment, gone the next.'

'Mum!'

'Like that precious greenfinch,' Mrs Carter said, 'flying straight into the window at breakfast. Whatever did it think it was doing?'

'Maybe it saw itself,' Annie suggested.

'I can't get it out of my head.'

'Mum,' said Annie, 'I'm going round Sandy's, to explain about last night.'

Mrs Carter nodded and closed her eyes. 'I'll come with you.'

Annie stiffened. 'It's all right.'

'I'll explain it was their last evening.'

'There's no need, Mum.'

'The walk will do me good,' Mrs Carter said. 'That'll clear my head.'

But when Annie and her mother reached the Boroffs' cottage, Sandy and Gracie were not at home. Sticking out of the letterbox was a white card with a message.

> *Out with Mom*
> *Fakenham.*
> *Same place, same time*
> *today—*
> *Sandy*

'What place, Annie?' her mother asked.
Annie didn't reply.
'Annie?'
'It's a secret.'
'Not the church.'
'No,' said Annie fiercely. 'Not the church.'

*   *   *

Late that afternoon, Annie asked her father whether she could borrow a couple of coils of rope he kept at the back of the potting-shed, the ropes he'd often used before his stroke. He'd tied their sideboard on to the top of the car and slowly driven it back from Baker's in Fakenham. And once, he'd tied himself to the cottage chimney while he was repointing it.
'Whatever for, girl?'
'Sandy and I need it.'
'You're not going climbing?'
'No, Dad.'
'Annie?'
'We're not! We've got to . . . secure something.'
Mr Carter knew better than to ask more

160

questions. 'You'll bring them back,' he said.

'I promise.'

'That costs, you know.'

What Annie didn't tell her father was that she also intended to borrow his old fishing gaff, the stick with the nasty-looking hook at one end that had once belonged to Mr Carter's grandfather and had his initials carved below the eye at the top of the handle.

'Where are you going, then?' Mrs Carter asked Annie at dinner.

'To meet Sandy.'

'I know that.'

'Mum!' complained Annie. 'First you want me to get out of your hair, and you tell me to rely on myself, and then when I do . . .'

'Don't you speak to me like that.'

'You'd hate it if I said I was bored.'

'You'd hate it, young lady, if I said you couldn't go out.'

Annie stood up. 'I'm going,' she said. 'I've got to.'

'Blast!' said Mr Carter. 'You're a wild cat, all right.'

'You be back before dark,' her mother warned her.

'Yes, Mum.'

As Annie left the cottage, she swiped the Carters' second torch from its place on the ledge under the telephone. In the potting-shed she shouldered the heavy ropes. Then she grabbed the gaff and set off for the Rectory garden.

Annie knew Sandy would be already waiting, and as likely as not, invisible. He has a way of sort-of melting into a place, she thought, so I can't see

161

him to begin with.

But Sandy appeared out of the weeping willow as soon as he saw Annie, and when she had slipped the heavy coils of rope off her right shoulder, she explained about having completely forgotten that it was Willa's and Storm's last night.

'There's one good thing, anyhow,' Sandy told her. 'My mom says Pitterpatter and his wife are meeting the council or whatever in the village hall this evening, so at least they're out of the way.'

At this moment, though, Annie and Sandy heard a loud scrunch-scrunch. Without a word, the two of them dived back behind the willow curtain.

Oh no! thought Annie. The rope. The gaff.

'Splendid!' exclaimed a man's voice. 'We're almost halfway there.'

'We'll get them,' a second, deeper voice growled. 'We'll get them all.'

Annie grabbed Sandy's arm. She rammed herself against him. 'Pitterpatter,' she breathed. 'Leppard.'

Sandy nodded.

'They've found the angels.'

'How do you know?'

'You heard them.'

'They could've been talking about the appeal,' whispered Sandy.

The Reverend Potter and Alan Leppard were so preoccupied that they didn't notice the ropes or the fishing gaff. Away they hurried down the gravel path and round the corner of the grey wall, and then Annie and Sandy heard the sound of a woman's voice and car doors slamming, and the crunch of tyres on gravel.

'Whew!' said Sandy.

162

'They've got them already,' cried Annie, and she sounded heartbroken. 'I know they have.'

'Not from the well, they haven't,' said Sandy. 'I laid these two crossed stakes over the top yesterday so I could tell if anyone had tried to go down, but they haven't.' Then Sandy produced a box of matches from one pocket of his shorts, and pulled a scrap of newspaper out of the other.

'What are you doing?' Annie asked him.

Sandy struck a match, lit one corner of the scrap of paper and dropped it into the well. At once, the seed of light began to spiral. Down and round, round and down.

Annie gazed at it, intently she followed it as if it were her last hope in this world. The light flowered; it flared, and then it went out. And in the silence, the well's darkness seemed to Annie even more dark, more thick, more bottomless than before.

'And the light shineth in darkness,' said Sandy. 'Isn't that what the Bible says?'

'Dunno,' Annie replied forlornly. 'It went out, anyhow.'

'You'll be all right,' said Sandy. 'You will.'

Annie didn't reply.

'I mean, I could if you want.'

For all that it was August, Annie could feel the chill from the well rising towards her. It was cool on her cheeks. She took a deep breath. 'I'd better get on with it,' she said. 'It's just, well, I've never done anything as dangerous as this.'

Annie stood up. She wound one end of the rope round her waist, and tied it with a reef knot. Then she threw the other end over the branch stretching above the well.

'Splicing and cleating and coiling and heaving,' recited Sandy under his breath. 'Jamming and slipping and kinking and sealing. Whipping and seizing. Rise and shine! There's always a knot at the end of the line.'

Annie grinned, but she felt nervous all right. 'Keep a tight hold of your end of the rope,' she instructed Sandy. 'I'll call up to you each time I want you to pay out a bit more.'

'OK,' said Sandy.

'But if a rung gives way . . . You won't be able to haul me up. You'll have to get help as quickly as you can.'

'OK,' said Sandy. 'I'll have to tie this end around the willow trunk first.'

'You might not be able to hear me,' Annie said, 'not when I'm right at the bottom. But as soon as you see the rope going slack . . .'

'I'll know you're coming up.'

'. . . yes, and you must pull it in and keep it taut.'

'OK,' said Sandy.

'Right!' said Annie. 'Now we'd better lower the gaff down first. I can't carry that as well as hold on to the rungs.'

'It's a good thing you brought the extra length of rope,' said Sandy.

As soon as Annie and Sandy had secured one end of the spare rope to the eye in the gaff handle and tied the other end to the overhanging willow branch, they lowered the gaff down into the darkness of the well.

'Right,' said Annie again. 'I've got my torch in this pocket, and I can hang it round my neck when I need to. I'm ready.'

'You're brave,' declared Sandy.

'I don't feel it.'

'I think you are.'

Annie swung herself over the coping and, facing the wall of the well, slowly let herself down.

'This rung's firm,' she reported. 'This first one, anyhow. Pay out the rope, Sandy. Three or four feet.'

Cautiously, Sandy paid out the rope, until Annie was holding the top rung and had planted both feet on the second one.

'Great!' Annie said. 'This one's OK, too! I'm going down now. Ready?' Her voice seemed to echo round and round her. 'Can you hear me all right?'

'Sort of.'

Rung by rung, Annie began to lower herself into the dark body of the well. Each time she tested a rung with one foot and then put her full weight on to it, Sandy paid out a little more rope; and each time Annie looked up, the eye of daylight grew smaller.

Annie could see the walls around her were black and slick. Piles of things must get blown down here, she thought. Leaves. Dead grass. Twigs. Insects. Birds, maybe. Frogs. And some stuff sticks to the walls, and then it rots and turns into a sort of black glue.

Down she went, Annie, rung by rusty rung. And when Sandy called to her, she could no longer make out what he was saying. His words sounded hollow in the well's throat, and made a nonsense of themselves.

'Speak . . . more . . . slow . . . ly!' Annie shouted.

Thirteen rungs . . . fourteen rungs . . . fifteen . . .

There's two feet between each rung, Annie said

to herself. What's twenty-two times two? I don't know. We don't do a twenty-two times table. Two twenties, that's forty. I'm more than forty feet under the Rectory garden. Whoever dug this well must have taken years and years.

I must almost be down to sea-level, thought Annie. Down, right down, where the whole world dissolves into water.

It stinks down here. It really does. The air's so thick it's hard to breathe. I keep coughing.

This was when Annie reached the water level. She stepped on to something soft.

At once Annie raised her foot again. She hooked her right arm over the rung, yanked the torch out of her pocket and hung it round her neck.

But when she turned it on, all she could see beneath her was a glutinous, oily mess, a crust of sticks, little bones, feathers, skeletons of leaves, all of them slightly swaying, and lying on it, her father's fishing gaff attached to the rope on which she and Sandy had lowered it. Around Annie, the walls were clammy, dark, and dripping. They're closing right in on me, she thought. They're trying to suffocate me. Squeezing me to death.

Annie screwed up her face. She reached down and grasped the gaff, and then she lowered herself through the revolting crust. The water was cold. It grabbed her ankles, her shins.

'Sandy!' yelled Annie. 'Water! Water!'

But her words exploded around her. They bounced right back into her head.

Annie gulped. Holding the iron rung that was just above water level, she lowered herself until the stagnant mess closed round her hips. She reached

166

down with the gaff as far as she could. And a little further . . . And that was when she touched the bottom.

Annie prodded it with her gaff. It was quite soft, soft yet firm. Mud, she thought. It must be.

When Annie reached for the rung above her head and tried to pull herself back out of the gripping water she realised her gaff was snagged. It wouldn't budge. She drove it down, twisting the hook a bit as she did so, and then tugged for a second time.

I've caught something, she thought. Not a fish. Not down here. Something big.

When Annie tugged for a third time, she was able to pull the gaff up towards her. Far above, Sandy was watching and waiting, and the moment he saw that the gaff rope had slackened, he started to pull it in over the branch of the weeping willow.

Annie's catch surfaced. A sack, is it, she thought. A tarpaulin? An Alsatian? No! Not a dead person. A dead baby. Please, no! It's not, is it?

Annie scarcely dared look but she looked. She couldn't tell what she had caught, not by the light of her swinging torch. She could see it was foul and slimy, and it was heavy.

It's not, thought Annie. It's not! Is it? It's too heavy. I'll have to wait until I get to the top. We'll have to pull it up together.

Annie was so out of breath, so nervous that she didn't even call up to Sandy. She just kept climbing, rung by rung, and as she did, Sandy kept the rope tight.

Above Annie's head, the white eye of daylight opened wider and wider.

'I can see you,' Sandy called down. 'The top of your head. Come on! Come on!'

But when Annie grasped the third rung from the top, it came right out of the wall. Annie screamed. She dangled, almost breathless, she swung and bumped her head on one side of the well. Then she found her footing on the rung below again.

'It's come out,' sobbed Annie.

'It's all right, Annie,' Sandy shouted. 'I've got you.'

'Quick!'

'Wait!'

And then Sandy did something he knew he would be proud of for the rest of his life. He secured the rope, wrapping it twice round the willow trunk; then he tied a loop in the end of it and lowered it down to Annie.

'Step into the loop,' Sandy told her. 'See if you can step into it and grab the rung above your head.'

'No,' panted Annie. 'I can't.'

'You can,' Sandy urged her. 'Come on! Put your foot into the loop. Even if you slip, you can't fall. You've still got the rope around your waist. I can take the strain.'

Then Annie took a deep breath and tried to step into the loop. But her foot slipped out of it and she was again left dangling, suspended by the rope around her waist.

'Nearly!' said Sandy. 'Try again.'

Annie did. And this time she stepped right into the loop, pulled herself up on her rope, and grabbed the rung over her head.

'Yeah!' bellowed Sandy. 'OK!'

Two more rungs and Annie was able to grasp

Sandy's outstretched hand. He pulled her up, up and over the coping.

Annie collapsed on to the grass beside the well, gasping. She gazed up at Sandy, wild-eyed.

'Boy!' said Sandy. 'I know you're a marsh-girl, a mud-girl, a wild girl, but this time . . .'

'You saved me, Sandy. You saved me. I was so scared. I wouldn't have been able to get out otherwise.' Annie was trembling, and several times she quivered.

'Right!' she said. 'The gaff-rope now.'

'Yeah. What have you got?'

'It's heavy. We'll have to pull it up together.'

'OK.'

'Hand over hand,' said Annie. 'Hand over hand.'

Together Annie and Sandy hauled up the gaff-rope, and then Annie grabbed her catch, she caught it in her arms and pulled it over the coping.

'Sewer-rat!' said Sandy, smiling. He picked up a garden stake and poked at Annie's catch.

'It's not!' gasped Annie. 'Is it?'

Sandy puckered his pale lips and watched the sack, or tarpaulin, or bundle of clothing or whatever it was oozing where he had punctured it.

'Might be,' he said.

'Oh!' Annie sat up on her elbows. 'I'm afraid.'

'Even if it's not . . .' Sandy began. 'Go on, then!'

Annie looked at Sandy under her dark eyelashes.

'Why me?'

'Because.'

'Because it's so revolting?'

'No,' protested Sandy. 'Because you . . . well . . . you started all this.'

Annie got on to her knees, feeling extremely shaky. And as soon as she tried to detach the gaff hook, it tore the sacking or flesh or whatever it was.

'Sacking,' said Annie. 'I think it is. I hope it is. Or else an old sheet or rug. There's something inside it.'

Then Annie used both hands. She pulled apart the filthy material.

Inside the sacking was something covered with black goo. Annie rubbed both her hands on the grass, and then she wiped the worst of the sticky ooze away.

And there! There, looking straight up at them, smutty-faced, was a smiling angel.

'Ohhh!' cried Annie and Sandy.

Then Sandy, too, got on to his knees.

Together they gazed down at the angel and their Waterslain angel gazed up at them.

The angel was lying on a nest of its own unhinged wings. It looked just like the one who had stood beside Annie's bed, and given her a piece of honeycomb and spoken to her, the angel who had sought and found her, and guarded her, in the saltmarsh.

22

For a while, less than two minutes, as long as their lives, Annie and Sandy knelt in silence beside the angel in the quietness of the Rectory garden.

After some time, Annie stood up and said, 'It's weird. I want to tell everyone, and yet at the same time I don't want to tell anyone, anyone at all.'

'That's because they're ours,' Sandy agreed. 'They're yours and mine and no one else's until we share them.'

'Yes,' said Annie, 'but they do belong to everyone in Waterslain.'

'They do,' said Sandy. He got to his feet. 'The quick and the dead. All the generations who raised their eyes and . . . and . . .'

'. . . and wished they weren't missing.'

'And wondered where they were.'

'Oh, Sandy!'

'So they belong to my dad, too,' Sandy said, 'these angels do. And he's one of them now, that's what my mom says. They're his comrades.'

Annie saw that the corners of Sandy's eyes were bright with tears.

'Anyhow,' said Sandy, 'telling everyone is the best way of stopping Leppard from getting his hands on them.'

'I can't wait to see his face,' said Annie.

'I'm going to be watching him closely,' Sandy told her. 'I want to see how he reacts.'

'We need help,' said Annie. 'Lots, actually. To bring all the others up.'

'Thirteen,' said Sandy.

'They're all down there. They must be.'

'Yeah!' cheered Sandy, raising both hands. 'We cracked it, Annie!'

Annie opened her arms and reached towards Sandy.

'Ugh!' Sandy exclaimed. 'You're as mucky as— as mucky as an angel.'

Then Annie lunged towards Sandy and threw her arms round him. 'So are you now,' she giggled.

'Ugh!' Sandy exclaimed again, squirming with delight.

'Mucky as angels,' Annie said. 'Both of us.'

*   *   *

The Reverend Potter heard the church hall door opening. He didn't bother to turn round.

'Come back after the meeting!' he boomed.

Annie and Sandy took no notice. They shoved the door open and sidestepped into the hall, carrying the foul, oozing bundle between them.

As they advanced on the long table, four members of the council stood up.

'Annie!'

'What is it?'

And then a horrified voice: 'It's not! It's not a . . . is it?'

The Reverend Potter turned round and eyed the disgusting cocoon. 'What do you think you're doing?' he demanded. 'We're right in the middle of our meeting.'

Annie and Sandy carefully lowered their bundle.

'Not on the floor,' screeched Mrs Potter. 'Daphne will have a fit.'

Annie and Sandy ignored her. They put down

their catch on the polished wooden floor. Then they stood up and faced Pitterpatter and Miss McQueen, the secretary, and Alan Leppard, and the other six members of the council.

Several of the councillors held their noses. Not one of them could take their eyes off the filthy, stinking whatever it was. The morass!

Without saying a word, Annie and Sandy stooped. Each of them took hold of one edge of the rotten material and gently raised it and folded it back.

In the quiet hall, the councillors caught their breath. One gave a sob; one a guttural gasp; one a sort of stifled shriek. Miss McQueen pressed her right hand against her purple lips; one man thought he was a boy again, and everything in the world was possible; the Reverend Potter felt as if he had stepped right into the manger in Bethlehem and was gazing down at baby Jesus. Sandy didn't take his eyes off Alan Leppard for one moment and, after a while, the garage-man returned his gaze with eyes as hard and unforgiving as flint; then he scowled angrily at Sandy and Annie.

The councillors edged closer. They stood in a ring round their angel and saw it smiling sweetly up at them. Then the quiet in the hall grew so wide and so deep—sky-wide, marsh-deep. Annie could hear her own breathing. Like that moment just after I wake up, she thought, before all my thoughts crowd in.

Then the questions began. And as Annie and Sandy told the amazing story of their summer quest, and Annie described how she had just climbed down into the well in the Rectory garden,

Sandy kept a careful watch on Pitterpatter and Alan Leppard. He saw the rector beaming and shaking his head. He saw Leppard scowling. He saw Pitterpatter's bristling right eyebrow jumping around. Then the garage-man gave Sandy the most burning, murderous look, as if he were about to tear him to pieces.

Sandy lowered his eyes. His pale skin flushed. We're right, he thought. We are, though we'll never be able to prove it. Anyhow, Leppard's too late. Annie and I got there first, and he can't do anything about it.

'Well, well!' the Reverend Potter exclaimed, and there was no mistaking it—he sounded blissful. 'Right under our noses! Right under our feet, all this time.'

'More than three hundred years,' murmured Miss McQueen.

Leppard glared at the angel. 'A couple of kids,' he muttered in disgust.

23

The Bishop of Norwich stood facing the people of Waterslain, wearing his mitre the colour of winter jasmine, holding his crook in his right hand.

It's the same shape as Dad's gaff, thought Annie. What's it for? Catching angels?

I was right and I was wrong. Alan was searching for the angels, all right, the same as we were, and we stopped him. We stopped him! If we hadn't, he'd have sold our angels. And if he'd been found out—well, he'd be in prison by now. But I was wrong to suspect Pitterpatter. He's not guilty at all. I don't know what got into me. Anyhow, it doesn't really matter now. Not any longer.

Annie and Sandy were sitting in the front row of the pews across the aisle from each other, and Willa and Storm and Mr and Mrs Carter were on Annie's left. Sandy was with his mother and his cousins from Lincoln and Josie Sidebottom. Each place in every single pew was occupied, and a fair number of people were swilling around in the gloom at the back of the church.

The two edges of the high hammerbeam roof were veiled with long ribs of scarlet cloth running the whole length of the church. Now and then, one of them rippled or trembled, or the other ballooned and then subsided, as if it were breathing.

The bishop turned to the Reverend Potter, and bowed his mitred head.

'We'll begin with a hymn,' announced Pitterpatter. 'Hymn four hundred and seventy-five.

4–7–5.'

'You do declare!' a voice called out, and a murmur of amusement ran through the body of the church. The corners of the bishop's mouth twitched.

'I do declare,' boomed Pitterpatter.

While the congregation sang, Annie remembered how Pitterpatter had summoned everyone to the church and told them about the appeal to replace their missing angels:

> *Ye holy angels bright*
> *Who wait at God's right hand . . .*

And she remembered how she saw Sandy staring at the inscription on the sunlit wall:

> *Or through the realms of light*
> *Fly at your Lord's command . . .*

She remembered Pitterpatter telling everyone about meeting her and Sandy on the marsh, and how she suspected him:

> *Assist our song,*
> *For else the theme*
> *Too high doth seem*
> *For mortal tongue . . .*

'Do sit down, everyone,' said the bishop. 'Now! It's not every day we gather to give thanks for a harvest of angels. Harvest? That's the wrong word. A shoal of angels.'

The Bishop of Norwich smiled. And when people in the village talked about him later, the

176

first thing many of them mentioned were his bright blue eyes; the way they sparkled; 'as if,' observed Miss McQueen, 'there were nothing for it but to laugh at life. Laugh and pray.'

'It's one year to the day,' the bishop said, 'one whole year since Annie and Sandy found your first angel. And what I want to say to begin with is how deeply grateful to them I am, and the Bishop of Lynn is.'

'As am I,' Pitterpatter chimed. 'And all of us here in Waterslain.'

'Indeed!' agreed the bishop. 'When you rang and told me that evening, I could scarcely believe my ears.'

That was the other thing about the bishop. His ears. He looks like a goblin or a pixie or something, thought Annie. His ears stick out at right angles.

'I came over next morning,' the bishop went on, 'and so did the Bishop of Lynn, and we saw the sweet angel Annie and Sandy had found; we saw eleven more angels rising from the well. For all of us who witnessed it, that was the most thrilling, the most inspiring day. Eleven angels, each in its own dripping, stinking . . . membrane. Well, almost eleven, to be absolutely accurate, because one angel was missing a left wing, the one found by Alan Leppard in the Reverend Potter's attic. Eleven angels, each of them drawn up with Tom Carter's old windlass.'

The bishop hesitated. 'It is Tom, isn't it?'

Tom Carter cleared his throat. 'Yes, your grace,' he muttered, and his blood rushed to his face.

'Yes,' the bishop continued, 'there's nothing Tom doesn't know about wells. And all the angels

177

were cat's-cradled down at the bottom by Mr Leppard. You were down there for more than three hours, weren't you, Alan?'

'Same as the service well,' Alan Leppard said. 'You know, down the garage.'

'Not the same at all,' the bishop replied with a smile. 'Servicing cars . . . saving angels. Well, I think we should thank these gentlemen, don't you?'

By way of a reply, everyone in the church clapped hard and long, and someone at the back whistled.

'So, we've found twelve angels,' said the bishop. 'I know there are fourteen pegs up in the roof. But the miracle is that we've found so many.'

Yes, thought Annie, and it's a miracle that they flew away before Smasher got them. Got them, and gutted them, and hacked them into pieces. He half-wrecked everything else in our church.

It was almost as if the bishop had read Annie's thoughts. 'Before we get any further,' he went on, 'we ought to remember the priest who hid our angels in his well, and left instructions where to find them. The Reverend Potter and I have had a careful look in the Black Book, and we believe his name was Martin Foulsham. Yes, let us remember him, and be thankful.

'Like most of you,' the bishop said, 'I saw your angels in the village hall, before they were hurried off to Cambridge to be pickled—or whatever it is scientists do with ancient wooden angels.' The bishop's blue eyes sparkled. 'What a sight! Twelve medieval angels propped up against the walls, filthy dirty. They were all covered in such grime you might have thought they were statues of

178

fishermen in black waterproofs and wellies. No, it wasn't until the restorers removed the grime that I could see what you're going to see—that five hundred years ago your woodcarver, John Chisel, gave each of your angels a very sweet smile . . . and two left feet!'

Annie felt her spine begin to tingle.

'We'll never know the reason,' the bishop continued. 'And I don't suppose most people will even notice. But anyhow, the restorers have left all the feet left, if you see what I mean.'

Annie couldn't stop shivering; she couldn't stop smiling.

The Bishop of Norwich waved towards the spry old woman sitting in the front pew, next to Gracie. 'Some of you may know Josie Sidebottom,' he said. 'And some of you will remember her nephew, Saricl Chisel. May he rest in peace. Josie lived here when she was a girl—she was a Groom—and so did Sariel until he and his parents emigrated to Australia. But do you all know that he was a descendant, a direct descendant of the John Chisel who carved your angels? Yes, the Chisels have lived in and around Waterslain for generations and generations.

'Not only this,' the bishop went on. 'There's something about the Chisels and wood—a sort of love affair. For generations, the family have been carpenters, bodgers, boat-builders, turners, carvers. Sitting next to Josie is another of her nephews, Peter. Peter Chisel. He works in the cathedral at Norwich, carving new limbs for worm-eaten saints and the like. That's how I know him, and I'm very happy to see him here today.

'Some of you have met Peter already,' the

bishop continued. 'Annie and Sandy have. Yes,' he said with a secret little smile, 'Peter was most particularly keen to see them for himself: the two children who found the angels carved by his own ancestor five hundred years ago.'

Annie leaned forward and looked across at Peter Chisel, and he winked at her. Actually, thought Annie, your face looks as if it's been hewn out of wood itself. All weathered and blocky and sharp-angled. Sort of unfinished. It's a wonder you can wink!

'I can't tell you anything about Annie and Sandy you don't already know,' the bishop said. 'I expect you've seen everything in the newspapers. Did you see that picture of Sandy being congratulated by all his classmates? Yes, in the newspapers, and even on television . . .' The bishop paused. 'I suppose you're expecting me to say something about what this all means. After all, that's what bishops are meant to do, isn't it? Yes, it's true, I could talk about friendship and intelligence and instinct and courage and persistence . . . all these things.'

Annie and Sandy didn't look at each other across the aisle, but they were joyfully, painfully aware of each other. Annie was trembling; and had she but known it, Sandy was trembling too.

'But instead . . .' the bishop continued. 'Well, the very reason we're all here today is to see your angels restored, your own angels come home, flown to their high perches. So I think they should sing for themselves.'

The Bishop of Norwich waved his left hand, and then he and the Reverend Potter proceeded to the opposite walls of the church and grasped the loose

180

ends of the two scarlet sashes hanging from the edges of the hammerbeam roof. Gently they pulled, and the ribs of cloth began to fall away, revealing the Waterslain angels. Pitterpatter and the bishop slowly paced down the church until almost all the cloth had come away from the roof.

In the body of the church, everyone looked up. A sea of pale faces. Almost like hundreds of water-lilies floating on the dark saucer of a pond. Then many people murmured like contented bees, and many stood up. A few even stood on the pews, so as to get just a little closer to their angels.

Soon everyone was talking, pointing, exclaiming, calling out . . .

All the vestments and wings of the twelve angels were vermilion and marsh-green and yellowy-orange once again, as they were in the beginning. And many of the angels were holding objects.

'A fishing net!'

'An oar!'

'A hayfork, look!'

'A sheaf of corn.'

'A black book.'

All around her, Annie could hear voices.

'They're helpers, the old angels are.'

'Helping us!'

'With their left feet and all!'

'It's . . . like . . . they never went away.'

'It that a girl or a boy, then?'

'Neither.'

'Both.'

Annie crossed the aisle, and Sandy turned to face her.

'They never did,' she said.

'What?'

'Go away. Nothing ever does—from Waterslain.'

'They would have done,' said Sandy, 'if we hadn't stopped Leppard.'

'We beat him!' said Annie. 'We did. And now he's . . . well, he's on the side of the angels. Helping Dad to bring them up.'

'And everyone's grateful to him,' added Sandy, shaking his head and smiling.

'I'm all out of breath,' Annie exclaimed.

Sandy gave her a watery smile. 'Again!' he said.

Side by side the two of them stared up into the roof.

'Each face is different,' Sandy said. 'Different features.'

'And each with a different kind of smile,' agreed Annie. 'Not like the ones at South Creake.'

'That one's got quite a crafty look,' Sandy said, 'and that one's surprised, and that one, with its mouth half-open, it's got a nervous smile.'

'And the one at the end there!' Annie added. 'Arms in the air! Like it's just scored a goal!'

'Except,' said Sandy, 'you can't play football with two left feet.'

Annie slowly shook her head. 'I knew the Wellingtons were a clue,' she said.

'Their colours though,' said Sandy, 'they're all the same. Like they really are a team. Peter Chisel says each colour means something.'

'They're the colours of this place,' Annie replied. 'That's what I think. Summer poppies, golden barley, the muddy green of the marsh.'

'Look, Annie,' said Sandy.

Annie looked.

And there, across the aisle, Mrs Carter and Gracie were laughing and hugging one another, and Tom Carter was standing next to them, grinning like a retriever.

Annie smiled. She smiled and smiled and for a moment she leaned against Sandy.

The Bishop of Norwich raised his crook, and slowly the hubbub around him subsided.

'So . . .' he began. And then more loudly, 'So!'

'Sshh!' hushed the congregation. 'Sshh!'

'So!' the bishop called out for the third time, 'Here are your high-fliers. Twelve of them. And that is almost the long and the short of it. The left and the left of it! The then and now of it.'

Then he and Pitterpatter pulled one last time on their sashes. In perfect unison, the lengths of cloth cascaded into two scarlet pools on to the tiled floor. They folded into themselves.

Once again, everyone looked up.

They looked and saw two angels facing one another across the nave of Waterslain church. One had a rather muddy face and was brandishing a fearsome gaff. The other angel was pale, almost pearly, and wearing thick-rimmed spectacles.